Claiming a Pirate
and
Submitting to the
Baron

by
EM BROWN

ISBN-13: 978-1-942822-15-8

OTHER WORKS BY EM BROWN

Cavern of Pleasure Series
Mastering the Marchioness
Conquering the Countess
Binding the Baroness
Lord Barclay's Seduction

Red Chrysanthemum Series
Master vs. Mistress
Master vs. Mistress: The Challenge Continues
Punishing Miss Primrose, Parts I - XX
Master vs. Temptress Trilogy
Wedding Night Submission

Chateau Debauchery Series
Submitting to the Rake
Submitting to Lord Rockwell
Submitting Again
Submitting to the Marquess

Other Novels
All Wrapped Up for Christmas
Force My Hand
A Soldier's Seduction

For more about these wickedly wanton stories,
visit www.EroticHistoricals.com

GOT HEAT?

"Ms. Brown has written a tantalizing tale full of hot sex...a very sexy and sometimes funny read that will definitely put a smile on your face."

– Coffee Time Romance review of
AN AMOROUS ACT

"Darcy's fierce, independent spirit and unconditional loyalty to her family will win readers over, and Broadmoor is a romantic hero to swoon for."

- RT Book Reviews on
FORCE MY HAND

"Sometimes you just pick up the right book that just hits you and makes you really love it. This was one of those books for me. I just got so into the story and never wanted it to end."

- Romancing the Book review of
SUBMITTING TO THE RAKE

"HOT AND FUN TO READ!!!!!!!!"

"This one made me go WOW! I read it in a few hours which technically I probably should have gotten more sleep, but for me it was that good that I deprived myself of sleep to finish this most awesome story!"

"...sex was intense...thrilling...."

"I loved this book. Clever dialogue that kept m[e] laughing, delightful characters and a wonderful story. I am not generally one who likes historical fiction but this book carried me along from page one."

TABLE OF CONTENTS

Claiming a Pirate

Chapter One

~ *The Golden Age* ~

Of all the ways to die, Adanya never thought it would be by sea. A blade through the heart by a traitorous crewman, perhaps. Swaying at the end of a hangman's noose, very likely. Old age, certainly. But not by sea. Not by the mistress she had feared and revered for nigh on three and ten years, since first she had been put to sea at the tender age of nine.

As she lay floating in her bateau with her breeches and shirt shredded, her salt-sprayed hair tangled and plastered about her bruised face, Adanya marveled at how serene the sea felt. Last night, the sea had heaved and pitched in fury as if in battle with the storm clouds above. Now a blue, cloudless sky stretched the length of the horizon, and the sea rolled and sighed like a satisfied lover who had just mended a quarrel.

She shielded her eyes from the glaring midday sun, but the movement made her ribs ache where grapeshot had skimmed her flesh. A dull throb persisted from the blow her quartermaster had dealt to her head, but she preferred these pains to the wrenching of her heart when she considered the fate of her ship, the *Sea Falcon*, and her crew.

"They'll hang us all—if we live," Adanya had shouted to her quartermaster, Damon, as a chain shot flew above them, tearing into the rigging. The *HMS Forte*, a fourth rate, had been battering the *Falcon* for over an hour, finding her aim despite the darkness of night.

Adanya meant her words, but an ugly doubt wormed through her. Not of Death. An early visit from that angel was inevitable for most pirates. And for her and the crew of the *Sea*

Falcon, they had all but made a pact with Death. She could almost relish dangling from Gallows Point, but more dreadful to her than the tar, feather and gibbets was the prospect that the British would not even dignify her with the fate of Charles Vane or Jack Rackham, perhaps choosing to burn her at the stake as if she were a common witch instead of the dread pirate who had amassed the largest collective bounty on her head.

"Or worse," she added beneath her breath, the words lost in the wind raging about them.

But Damon seemed to hear it nonetheless and, despite the darkness, she saw clearly in his eyes that he would sooner lie at the bottom of the sea than be sold back into slavery—a sentiment shared, no doubt, by the rest of her crew.

"What now, Cap'n?" Damon demanded.

Like her, he would betray no fear. She scanned her crew — all dedicated, all family to her. They, and the purpose that propelled her reason to live, had done much to relieve the hollow left by one Dominic Bold.

The wind, behaving like a wild banshee, howled at her, throwing droplets of rain into her face that stung like pellets of stone. But the storm was the least of their concerns. They had as many men at the pumps as could be had and still the *Falcon* was taking in water. The *Forte* was pulling up on the starboard side. Within half an hour, His Majesty's Navy would be boarding the *Falcon.* Their small but mighty crew would be no match for the number of men aboard the *Forte.*

"We fight," she declared to Damon, drawing her cutlass and biting back the burst of pain at her side.

Damon grunted. "Ye can escape, Cap'n. We can hold 'em off. Ye can sail off in a bateau. They'll not see you in the dark."

Adanya shot Damon an admonishing glare. "I would sooner writhe in Davey Jones' locker than live a coward to watch my brothers die."

"We reckoned that to be our fate when we joined ye" Damon shouted. "If ye lived, ye can assemble a new crew. Find a new ship. Carry on the dream of yer father."

For a moment, Adanya hesitated. Was she being selfish for

wanting to die in the comforting company of her crew? Vain for not wanting to be a coward? Weak because the prospect of starting anew daunted her? Was she already a coward for knowing that she could not bear the grief she would suffer, were she to survive and all else perished, leaving her an empty shell whose bowels had been ripped from her? She had no wish to die alone and in such a state.

"I go down with the ship, Damon," she said. "Have the men find whatever weaponry they can."

She turned to shed her coat. The garment, weighted by rain, would hinder her in close combat.

"Sorry, Cap'n."

Damon had mumbled the words, and before she could ascertain what he meant, she was thrown into a deeper darkness.

* * * * *

The sun peered over the horizon, its glow bringing the promise of another warm day. She had spent the previous day drifting in a daze. Adanya eyed the apparition of a ship in the distance. Already she was suffering delusions. What were the chances the *Sea Falcon* had escaped the *HMS Forte*? The *Falcon* was one of the fastest ships but had sustained heavy damage.

The hull of the ship advancing towards her was too wide to be the *Falcon*, the tonnage not enough to be the *Forte*. Perhaps it wasn't a mirage. Adanya sat up.

A schooner. Even without full sails unfurled in all her glory, the approaching vessel had grandeur to her. Adanya admired the ship, from the tip of the bowsprit to the top of its mainmast. No flags flew from its mast tops. No pendants. Then it wasn't a war ship. Perhaps a privateer.

Or...another pirate.

Making out the figurehead, Adanya fell back onto the planks with a groan, willing the sea to swallow her whole at that moment.

Of all the miserable luck. Of all the people, it had to be *him*.

She heard rather than saw the ship pulling abreast. And though nearly five years had passed, a voice more familiar than her own reached her ears.

"Well, well...Captain Mbwana."

She could hear the grin in the way he spoke. She kept her eyes closed, as if hoping to wake to a different fate.

"Would you be needin' a hand?"

Her eyes snapped open to find a pair of dark eyes laced with mirth gazing down at her. Damn. Dominic Bold was as handsome as she last remembered—mayhap more.

The sun's rays played on his auburn hair with russet glints. Dressed in a blue coat with trim, the top buttons of his shirt undone to reveal the muscular ridges of his chest, and with but two days' growth of beard on his rugged chin, he looked particularly refreshed and debonair. Dominic had always looked half gentleman, half pirate. She was struck by how miserable she must have looked in comparison.

"Only a fool need ask," she called back as she rose to her feet and reached into the water for the rope that had been thrown down the side of the ship for her.

"'Tis an honor to have the illustrious Captain Mbwana aboard the *Phantom*," Dominic said once two of his crew had hauled her onto the deck. He bowed with a grandeur befitting a king's court.

Adanya moved her gaze from the muscular leg he presented up the length of his broad chest and shoulders. When she met his eyes, the half-smile on his face indicated he had seen her appreciative sweep of his body.

She quickly changed her focus to the ship. Except for the addition of another square topsail, a new topgallant on her foremast, and new faces among the crew, the *Phantom* looked much as it did the last time she had been aboard. She found comfort in the familiarity, and as much as he unsettled her, there was comfort in Dominic as well.

She was handed a flask of water, which she tried not to swig too swiftly in her thirst.

"I shall have our quartermaster arrange a cabin for you," Dominic informed her. "It won't be what you're accustomed to—"

"Anything will do, thank ye," Adanya said. She almost reminded him of where she used to sleep—with the crew of the *Phantom*—but decided not to bring up the past. She did not trust herself to venture there, and she could not decide if she was relieved or hurt that he could muster such a blithe tone, as if they were about to sit down to bloody tea, as if they did not share a past.

"I take it you won't be needin' your, er, vessel?" he inquired.

Adanya looked down at the bateau that had served as her home for the last two days. An ache filled her heart. What if that was all that remained of the *Sea Falcon*?

As if reading her mind, Dominic dropped his humor and said, "We passed her a day ago, a British warship in pursuit but losing ground by the hour. That were a fine fast ship you have."

Relief flooded her—and then a swelling of pride. He approved of her ship. The smile on his lips indicated he was glad to be the bearer of good news.

She felt a sudden urge to bring those lips down upon her own.

An uneasy warmth surged in her loins as she recalled how it once felt to have his mouth consume hers. Their gazes connected, and suddenly it seemed as if they were the only two people in the world and five years had melted into none.

"Captain Bold?"

Adanya looked past Dominic to find the source of the sweet, feminine voice was a beautiful redheaded woman, wearing a yellow and ivory gown that displayed slender sloping shoulders and a small waist. With alabaster skin, rouged cheeks, and soft and supple flesh, the woman was the mirror opposite of Adanya, whose years of working on a ship had further darkened her ebony skin and hardened her flesh into toned muscle.

"I see you've not given up your taste for wenches," Adanya noted, trying to keep the jealousy out of her voice. She licked her own chapped lips to make them less unsightly before the rosy lips of the other woman.

"Old habits die hard—or not at all," Dominic replied. He

turned to the gentlewoman. "Miss Wrenwood, I present to you Captain Adanya Mbwana."

Miss Wrenwood bobbed a curtsy. "Pleased to meet you, sir."

Adanya stiffened, though she could not fault the woman for thinking her a man. Not only was she dressed in a shirt and breeches, but her bosom, as was her custom, was bound to disguise her form. Her crew knew her to be a woman, but they did not need reminders of her womanhood.

"Captain Mbwana has the current honor of being the scourge of the Atlantic," Dominic praised. "The English have placed a bounty on her head of no less than twenty thousand quid."

"Her?" Miss Wrenwood echoed, her eyes searching Adanya with obvious doubt.

"Surely the bounty on *your* head differs little," Adanya returned graciously.

"Alas, I am told that I am worth but five thousand nowadays."

"Then," said Miss Wrenwood to Dominic, "he—she, is a pirate as well?"

This time Adanya bowed but kept her gaze on Dominic. "I learned from the best, m'lady."

"Too well," Dominic replied with foreboding. He turned to a bearded man he addressed as Mr. Collins and told him to set an extra place at the captain's table for supper.

"My first mate will see you to your quarters," Dominic said to Adanya.

"Rowland Stirling, at your service," greeted a tall man with soft hair and icy blue eyes.

The first mate was almost as attractive as Dominic, but in Adanya's eyes, Dominic was a near perfect specimen of man, being a perfect blend of his mother and father. Dominic's dark eyes and full lashes came from his French mother, a beautiful woman whose portraiture Adanya had seen in Dominic's cabin. The broad shoulders, expansive chest, and skin that bronzed easily in the sun Dominic inherited from his father, a Mongol pirate.

Dominic bowed, then offered his arm to Miss Wrenwood

and led her away. Adanya watched their departing backs. She wanted to retch.

"I shall have a set of clothes brought to you," Rowland said as he showed Adanya below deck and opened the door to a small but well-lighted cabin. "I am sure Miss Wrenwood would spare a gown—"

"I've not worn a gown but once in me life," Adanya interrupted, "and no desire to do so again."

It wasn't entirely true. She could well remember the way Dominic had looked at her that day she had dug up a gown from a recent pillage. He had looked at her differently, no longer as his pilot, but as a *woman*. Adanya would have given anything to see his eyes light up in the same manner once more.

But gown or not, she knew she could not hold sway over his attentions as well as the likes of Miss Wrenwood. She imagined Dominic running his hands through Miss Wrenwood's long silken tresses. He could not do the same with her motley hair.

And to her horror, she felt the tentacles of jealousy gripping her once more. How she loathed that feeling. Five years should have squelched such sentiments.

"Be you wantin' anything...?" Rowland asked with a restrained but eerie eagerness. His eyes bore into her as if he sought to unearth her secrets.

"Nay," Adanya replied, meeting his stare. Rowland would be a devilishly handsome man but for the subtle sneer upon his lips. He wore his light brown hair streaked with flaxen in a loose queue, a single earring of gold through an ear, and two pistols at his sides. She wondered why the man armed himself when walking about his own ship and imagined he was the kind to sleep with one eye open. A man who trusted no one could not himself be trusted.

She went to stand by the door, waiting for him to leave. He smiled—to her or himself, she knew not, but cared little that he should find amusement in her.

"If there be anything," he said as he stepped outside, "we are at your service."

He began an awkward bow, but he lacked the grace that

Dominic, a man of many worlds, could conjure. She shut the door in the middle of his bow.

Alone, she sat down on her bed and released the groans and grimaces that she, not wanting to reveal the slightest weakness before Dominic, had forced inside. She put her head in her hands. She had to find a way back to her ship.

But most of all, she had to get away from Dominic and all the terrible wrenching feelings that knotted her guts whenever her gaze met his. His tone had been lighthearted enough, but she knew he had not buried the past any more than she had.

Chapter Two

Y ou mock me, Captain Bold. She is no pirate captain," said Sarah Wrenwood as she walked Dominic back to his cabin. "I never heard of a woman pirate."

Dominic looked into her large green eyes, fringed with thick golden lashes. The daughter of a wealthy merchant, Miss Wrenwood had been sailing on a ship bound for South Carolina when it had been overtaken by the *Phantom.* His gaze dropped to her gloved hands carrying a white-lace parasol. Miss Wrenwood was unlikely to have worked a day in her life, let alone experienced the harshness of a life at sea. And though she now found herself a captive aboard a pirate's ship, Dominic had allowed her many more comforts than he granted his own crew.

"In China, you'd find women pirates have existed for centuries."

"How barbaric."

"Or have you never heard of Anne Bonny or Mary Read?"

"I can't imagine why a woman would want to take to piracy." Sarah shuddered. "This Captain Moo-wana must be a dreadful person."

"Mbwana. A dread pirate, yes. A dreadful person, no."

Miss Wrenwood narrowed her eyes at him. "You know her?"

Not wanting to explain the past, he faced her with a grin. "Are you jealous, m'lady?"

She quickly flushed and snapped, "Of course not! What is there to be jealous of? I can hardly wait to rid myself of your company."

He stepped towards her, backing her up against the wall. "Your screams in my bed last night would indicate otherwise."

"You are a rogue, Captain Bold!" She shook her head and

tore herself away from him.

Dominic watched her indignantly arched back disappear up the steps to the deck. As much as he would have liked to prove her lie further by grabbing her and kissing her until she whimpered, he was more grateful for the solitude at the moment.

Entering his cabin, he made straight for the sideboard to pour himself a shot of whiskey. He did not believe in Providence or Fate, but what were the chances that he would come upon *her*—in the middle of the ocean—if not by the hand of some greater design?

His crew had detected the battle between the *HMS Forte* and *Sea Falcon* from a league away, and in a rare fit of curiosity, Dominic had ordered the *Phantom* closer. When at last he spotted the flag of the *Sea Falcon* through the telescope, he'd felt his stomach plummet. He had never seen the Jolly Roger of the *Falcon*, but he knew the skull and shackles to be hers. It must have galled Adanya to no end that she was being rescued by him, Dominic thought with satisfaction.

The poor thing had looked a miserable wreck.

And magnificent.

The mantle of captain hung about her well. She had always been a little defiant, a little arrogant, but now her arrogance had true deeds to prove her confidence was not misplaced. She had always possessed fortitude—he had seen it instantly that day he had plucked her off a slave ship when she had been a mere urchin not ten years of age. She had survived the ghastly voyage where many others had perished.

Trading his glass for the entire bottle, Dominic threw himself into his armchair and propped his heavy boots on the footstool. Their initial meeting had not been auspicious. Wielding a sling shot she had stolen from the cabin boy, she had launched a stone at his groin. It was the first slave ship he had ever attacked, having thought it to be a merchant ship carrying finished goods.

The *Bountiful.*

He remembered the ship well, for it carried with it the most horrific stench—a mixture of the urine, feces, and unwashed bodies of over six hundred men, women, and children crammed head to toe, filling every inch of space such that they could not stretch their legs nor lie down to sleep. The emptiness in their penetrating eyes made them appear something other than human.

The sunlight crept far enough into the hold for him to see one woman in particular, her eyes swollen shut, her cheeks blackened and crusted. He would later learn from Mbwana, Adanya's father, that the woman had refused to eat, choosing to starve to death. To force her mouth open, the crew of the *Bountiful* had burned her with hot coals.

"We're not taking a bloody thing from this cursed ship," Dominic had told his quartermaster, a small, sinewy man named Ponso, after scrambling from the hold back onto the deck to take a much-needed gulp of fresh air. He could not bear staring into all those ghostly eyes any longer.

Even Ali, his first mate, an Arab who had seen the most grotesque of atrocities in his lifetime as a pirate in the Red Sea, had emerged from the hold with a frown.

"Round the crew back onto the *Phantom*," Dominic had instructed.

Unlike Ali, who always seemed to know Dominic's wishes before he even spoke and tarried not even half a second before going to execute the orders, Ponso had remained where he was. "But Cap'n, the men be expectin' a prize. This cargo can fetch a fine sum."

"I don't bloody care."

Ponso twisted his long bony fingers, clearly not wishing to give up the bounty. "Should we not put it to vote?"

Dominic collared the man and pulled him in until they were nose to nose. "You sail on my ship, Ponso. My ship, my orders."

He was about to explain that he would give up his share of future bounties when he glanced past Ponso to a little girl standing a few yards away. She had thick lips and eyebrows that arched over a pair of deep, intense eyes, made all the more striking by the profound grooves of her eyelids.

He felt a sudden odd sense of shared destiny with the girl— and then his scrotum seemed to explode.

He doubled over and fell to his knees, his sword clattering to the deck.

Biting back a howl of pain, he looked up to see a sailor from the *Bountiful* falling upon him with an axe and certain death. He could not reach his sword in time. Nor could he pull his pistol from his belt, cock it, aim and fire.

A dark body flew before his eyes, colliding with the sailor. The two bodies landed on the deck. The man on top was a blackamoor—one of the slaves. Before the *Bountiful* sailor could raise his axe against his assailant, a long dagger was plunged into his throat.

Dominic grabbed his sword and scurried to his feet. Sword in hand, he faced the blackamoor, who had also risen. Despite having been on what was no doubt minimal nourishment, the slave was an imposing specimen of man, his carriage as regal as that of a prince.

They had stared at one another in tense silence before Dominic had finally lowered his sword. They had spoken no words, yet had come to an understanding. That became the way between Dominic and Mbwana. When Mbwana had indicated he wished to join Dominic instead of returning to the Ivory Coast with the other slaves, Dominic had agreed without qualm. The girl, however, Mbwana's daughter, had been another matter. A woman—a child—had no place on a pirate's ship, but Dominic could not refuse the man who had saved his life.

He should have listened to his gut, Dominic recalled as he downed another gulp of whiskey in the quiet of his cabin, relishing the way the liquid burned down his throat. He knew then a woman onboard meant trouble—he simply had not known that she would be trouble for *him*.

After Adanya had deserted him five years ago, he had vowed never to have a woman aboard who was not a captive being held for ransom. He would not even allow the strumpets at port to tour the ship. Now *she* was back aboard his ship, and it was half a fortnight at full sail to the closest land. He did not know where the *Sea Falcon* made berth. And he would need to be mindful of the *HMS Forte*.

What was he going to do with Captain Mbwana—Adanya—for a whole sennight?

What he wanted to do was tear off her clothes and fuck her. Fuck her hard. Fuck her until she cried. Until she asked his pardon for what she had done. And then he wanted to worship her in his arms. With all the passion and desperate longing locked inside him.

Dominic threw the now-empty bottle of whiskey at the fireplace, where it shattered into pieces. His cock stretched painfully against his breeches. Where had Miss Wrenwood stormed off to when he needed her?

He unbuttoned his pants, grabbed his cock and pulled at it.

It had been five fucking years. And though he had followed her exploits with interest—was decidedly proud to learn that she had become captain of her own ship—Adanya should have faded to a distant memory. There had certainly been more than enough women between the years. She hadn't even been the best tumble he had ever had.

He remembered how awkward she had appeared in that gown. He had never seen her in one before. Aboard the slave ship, she had been permitted only a loincloth though her breasts had been well on their way to womanhood. When she had come to live aboard the *Phantom*, there were only shirts, breeches and boots to offer her. Dominic wasn't even sure where the gown had come from. Most likely from a recent pillage.

Not surprisingly, the dress had looked all wrong on Adanya. It had been too small, for one. The back of the gold taffeta dress remained open, possibly because the pins could not keep it closed. The stays barely laced—he wondered who in the world could have helped her with those and was amused to think it might have been Mr. Withers, the ship's cook, for that kindly older man could never refuse Adanya anything.

The dress had hung like a deflated balloon about her hips, for she had neglected the panniers and petticoats. Her round, ripe breasts were bursting against the bodice. And beneath the ensemble, she wore her black leather bucket boots.

Reviewing the divisions his quartermaster had

recommended on their latest booty, Dominic had been seated at his writing desk when Adanya had knocked on his cabin door and requested to speak to him. She had become his pilot a year ago at a tender age of six or seven and ten, for her sea acumen was nearly unparalleled. As a child, she'd had a voracious appetite for learning anything and was forever at his side or that of his boatswain. Roughly ten years her senior, Dominic had come to regard her almost as if she were his own son.

"What the devil are you wearing?" Dominic had demanded.

Adanya seemed taken aback, and Dominic instantly regretted the edge in his tone. But then she became affronted. "'Tis a dress, or can't you bloody tell?"

"I know 'tis a bloody dress," Dominic responded. He would not have tolerated such insolence from any other crew member, but for some reason he could never bring himself to punish Adanya. "Why are you wearing it?"

She shrugged her shoulders. "Wanted to see what it felt like."

"It's not proper attire for the pilot of my ship," he told her, and turned to review the coordinates she presented so that she wouldn't find him staring at her bosom, sure that her nipples would spring out over the top of the décolletage at any moment. "Why are we traveling so far south when our destination lies due west?"

"Because the stream pushing east is strongest at that latitude. It were quicker taking a southern route."

"Very well," he said, handing the navigation map back to her.

She took the map but did not turn to leave. She bit her bottom lip and fidgeted with the map in her hands.

"What is it?" he asked, tilting his chair as he reached his arm back for his quill.

"Will you lay with me?"

He fell out of his chair.

After scrambling to his feet, he looked at her through narrowed eyes. She stared back with those bright, wide eyes of hers, the whites of which he could always find in the darkness.

"Have you been drinking foul beer?" he demanded, though

he knew the answer. Any beer aboard the ship had been exhausted already.

Adanya flushed but pressed her lips together in determination. She sounded exasperated when she spoke. "Will you?"

It was absurd. But absurdity what was gotten when one took a woman aboard a ship.

"Your father would kill me were he still alive—nay, he would flay the skin from my bones and dig out my eyes before hanging me from the yard by my scalp." Dominic hoped that would put an end to the matter.

"Well, he ain't alive," said Adanya in a low voice.

Damnation. Dominic ran a hand through his hair. Why him? There was any number of men among his crew who would have gladly gone at her quim. Only they knew if Mbwana didn't kill them, he would. Tumbling a willing female captive was one thing. Consorting with a fellow crew member was another. He would never have had to face such a problem if he hadn't been a damned fool to take on a woman in the first place.

"Am I not fair enough?"

Again her words cut at him more sharply than her smallsword. He turned to face her—and it dawned on him that she was a *woman*.

As one who had known all manner of women, from older, seasoned matrons to young, guileless maids, and who had come to learn all the chicanery, seduction, coquetry and tribulations employed by that most damnable, desirable and devastating sex, he had somehow overlooked the one and only woman he set eyes on every day. Beyond the shirts and breeches that he was accustomed to seeing Adanya in, beyond her role as his pilot and a member of his crew, beat the heart of one who was clearly of the tender sex.

"I know I haven't the dove-white skin, nor them ruby lips, or flaxen hair—"

Dominic looked down at her with softened eyes. "You're worth more than all of them put together."

"Then why will you not lay with me?"

"Because you're my pilot," Dominic replied firmly. He felt

uncomfortably warm, and his cabin felt as if it had shrunk in size.

"I'm a woman."

"Aye—a mistake I don't mean to ever make again." He saw a flash of hurt in her eyes, so he decided to change his tact. "Why would you wish me to bed you?"

"I see how they look at you—them women you take captive for ransom. Even the whores in the ports. I—I hear them scream...in pleasure, like."

This time it was Dominic's turn to flush. Again, if his crew had been all male, he would not be facing this situation.

"I want to know what 'tis like," Adanya finished. She stepped towards him, covering the distance between them, her thick black lashes lowered. "What is it like to give and receive such pleasure?"

When she looked up at him with those brown doe-like eyes, Dominic knew he was about to make the second biggest mistake of his life.

Chapter Three

The knocking at his door prompted Dominic from his chair. He grabbed the nearest piece of linen and wiped the seed from his cock before buttoning his breeches. His release had not brought about the relief he had sought. Still agitated, he made a note to himself to ensure that Miss Wrenwood stayed after supper.

"What is it, Mr. Robbins?" Dominic asked after he had opened his door to greet his ship's surgeon.

"You asked for a report of Captain Mbwana," said the young, slender man, adjusting the spectacles perched atop his nose. "She seems to be in a fair way."

"Seems? Did you not examine her?"

"Well, she—Captain Mbwana would not consent to my examining her."

Dominic pressed his lips in a firm line. Why was he not surprised?

"Come with me," he directed the surgeon.

"She was quite insistent on the matter," Mr. Robbins added as he scurried after Dominic.

"As am I, Mr. Robbins."

Dominic marched down the corridor to Adanya's cabin and opened the door.

A dagger flashed in the corner of his eye. He let out an oath as he ducked away from the blade.

"What the bloody hell was that for?" he asked.

"Didn't know it was ye, Captain," Adanya replied, returning her dagger to the hilt strapped around her thigh. "Perhaps ye should try knockin'."

"This is my ship, and I go wherever I please," said Dominic. "The doctor here will see to your wounds."

"I've no need of a doctor. Where is Dumaka?"

"Dumaka was no doctor, his practice little more than poor attempts at witchcraft."

"I know not your doctor."

"You've no need to know him," Dominic said, his patience wearing thin. "You will allow Mr. Robbins to tend to you."

"I thought I was an honored guest?"

"Ignore me again and you can be my honored captive instead."

Now it was her gaze casting daggers at him, but Dominic held his ground. Five years had given him the ability to do that, at least.

Without a word, she sat down on the bed and allowed Robbins to approach. The doctor looked at the cuts and bruises upon her face, into her eyes, her throat. He then examined a laceration he saw through a tear in her shirt. He cleared his throat and mumbled, "To, er, assess the wound better, er, the clothes—"

Adanya snapped away from the doctor.

Leaning against the doorframe with his arms crossing his chest, Dominic raised his eyebrows at her as if she were a wayward child disobeying orders.

"You wouldn't want me to remove the clothes on your behalf," Dominic informed her, though he would have been more than happy to carry out his threat.

With obvious reluctance, Adanya pulled off her shirt and removed the bindings about her chest. Though bearing lines from the linen that held them captive, her breasts nonetheless looked glorious. Dominic willed his cock to remain where it was while he eyed the large brown areolas. God help him, if the doctor were not present...

"I noticed you wince earlier when you reached over," Robbins said to Adanya as he examined the wound at her side, just below her breast, blackened and encrusted by blood. The skin had been torn or burned off in parts, exposing the bright pink flesh beneath. Dominic marveled at her stoicism.

Robbins felt gently about her ribs. "There appear to be no broken bones. I will fetch you some bandages and make a poultice for your wounds to ward against infection."

"Thank ye, doctor," Adanya mumbled.

When she looked up to glare at Dominic, he could not help a small smile, relishing her discomfort. She merited much more from him.

Her gaze went past him, and Dominic turned to find his first mate staring at Adanya. How long had Rowland been standing there?

"I found some clothes," Rowland said when he realized he was the focus of attention. "They must have belonged to the cabin boy who sailed on the ship with Miss Wrenwood."

Dominic took the clothes and tossed them to Adanya. As much as he wanted to stay and watch Adanya dress, he left with the doctor and Rowland.

"If she presents you with any more difficulties," Dominic said to Robbins, "you have but to inform me."

The doctor nodded his head, but Rowland felt no compunction to leave matters alone.

"You knew her," Rowland said.

"As did half my crew," Dominic replied. He had even less desire to share his past with Rowland than with Miss Wrenwood, especially after seeing the look Rowland had cast at Adanya. The tenting at the man's crotch did not escape his notice either. "She was the best pilot the *Phantom* ever knew."

She had had more flesh when she'd served aboard the *Phantom*, Dominic noted. Though he preferred her a little more rounded, he still found her body no less marvelous. It was like a sleek sloop, with strength and substance. He could see her shapely legs through the breeches she wore, and his mouth watered at her high and fleshy arse. Women with arses like hers should never be allowed to wear breeches. It taunted and begged to be taken.

"Did you—" Rowland began.

Dominic turned to his first mate to put an end to any more inquiries. "I'll see you at supper. And have Miss Wrenwood sent to my cabin—now."

* * * * *

Adanya stared at the clothes Rowland had brought. For a brief moment, despite what she had told the man, she wondered at wearing a gown.

But that would be madness. Floating in the sea had gone to her head. Did she think she could compare to the likes of Miss Wrenwood? She must have appeared to Dominic that first night as pitiable as a sick pup, looking no less ridiculous than a carnival animal in that ill-fitting gown.

And yet, he had made her feel like a queen. She still felt a sense of triumph that she, *she* had somehow managed to seduce Captain Bold into taking her into his bed.

"There will be pain," he had warned her. "Intense pain when your maidenhead is breached."

His words of caution had not daunted her. How bad could the pain be? Surely not as bad as when she fell from the ship rigging and broke her arm against the fore boom? Or when she and half the crew had fallen ill from drinking a keg of infested rum, their bowels feeling as if they were being twisted from the inside out?

Cupping her chin, Captain Bold had lowered his head, his eyes searching her face. She remembered how the flame of the lantern illuminated the blacks of his eyes, how the blood pulsed in her veins at his nearness.

"Are you certain you want this?" he asked with a softness she had only heard once from him. She had been ten years or so in age, and her father had been badly wounded in an attack against an East Indiaman. Adanya had feared for his life. Worried that her father would hear her cry, she had left his bedside and gone above deck. Captain Bold had found her hunched over her knees in the crow's nest. She did not remember his words—indeed, he had stumbled over them for it clearly was not a habit of his to console anyone, let alone a child—but his tone had comforted her nonetheless. They had sat in that crow's nest for what seemed hours. And she had never felt safer.

This time his husky voice evoked feelings of a different nature—a warmth, a yearning, and a thrill that made her breath catch in her throat. She saw the hesitation in his eyes, and before he could withdraw, she reached up and pulled his mouth down to hers. She had no notion of how to kiss a man, but she had seen many men—the Captain included—plant their lips on women. She had found such a custom strange at first, but with the pressure of Captain Bold's lips on hers, she began to understand.

It was the grandest of sensations. Heat flared through her loins. She wanted more. As much of him as she could take. Her hips pressed to him of their own accord.

After an initial moment of surprise, he responded. His mouth bore down on her, engulfing her, consuming her lips. Her head spun. What was she to do? All that she had learned— how to aim a pistol, how to cut a man to deliver the most potent strike—provided no defense for her now. But she soon realized there was little she need do. He dictated what took place, if her mouth should be closed or open, if she should move or remain still. He cupped the back of her head while his mouth devoured her. She felt his strength as much as she did the times he would throw off his coat and join his men in tying down the rigging or unloading the cargo.

How often had she made an effort to appear larger and stronger than she was? Once, in an attempt to disprove the weakness of her sex, she had insisted on assisting with the securing of a heavy canon. But the weight proved too much for her. She could not hold on to the ropes, and the cannon rolled over the toes of one of the mates.

But in Dominic's arms, she did not have to fight off the weakness she felt. Indeed, she would not have done so even if she could. His touch had a potency greater, more fiery than the stiffest of drinks. She feared the flame would burn inside of her forever. She did her best to quell it by partaking of his mouth as readily as he did of hers. Strangely, the heat only grew and deepened inside her belly.

After roaming his mouth over hers, he lightened his touch. Afraid he intended to withdraw, she grasped the lapels of his coat and pulled him closer. His kiss returned to its prior fervor, and his tongue delved between her lips, seeking hers. Is this what he did with all the women? But of course he did. The rapture of it explained why they all wanted more of his company, why it seemed they would do anything for him. But did all men and women engage in the joining of lips?

How fine he tasted! Cakes of ripened plantains could not compare. Even if she had consumed naught but slabber-sauce before tasting of sugar-covered yams, nothing could be more heavenly than the assault she suffered.

His hand dropped to her neck, and she started, for it was a most vulnerable part of her. She would never have allowed anyone but her father to touch her there. But when Dominic wrapped his other arm about her waist, her wariness melted. She knew she was safe with Dominic.

He kissed as if he meant to take her every breath. She could not contain the fervor, the desperate yearning of her body, and eagerly pushed herself into him. Surprised, he stumbled in the direction of his bed, but before they fell, he turned so that he landed atop her. The weight of his body sent her into madness. She wrapped a leg over him and bucked her hips vigorously. It was what she had seen the whores in port do.

He pulled back, and to her consternation, laughed.

"What?" she demanded.

"There are many courses to the repast."

What the devil did he mean by that?

He reached around for her leg. His hand went beneath the skirts and touched her bare calf. It was madness how his caress lit her body on fire and sent shivers through her. His hand slid up her calf to the back of her knee, and she bowed off the bed, her breasts bumping into his chest. Her breath grew haggard. He was looking at her, gauging her reaction. She wanted to affirm that this was what she wanted, but she was lost in the brilliance of his eyes. His hand continued its journey up her leg and came to rest on her outer thigh. Desire pulse between her legs.

"Kiss me again," she said.

Lowering his head, he did as she bid and brushed his lips over hers. It was a softer kiss but thrilled no less. Had she known such enchantment existed, she would have attempted to seduce Dominic earlier. She forgot what the women did, if anything, or what they said.

She had witnessed Dominic in congress on three separate occasions. The first had been by chance when she was taking a piss in the shrubs. The crew had been camped upon the beach in Nassau. Hiding behind the foliage, she had stood transfixed at what she saw and heard. At first, she had thought the woman writhing between Dominic and the palm tree to be in pain. Only later, upon seeing how the whore smiled and would not leave his side, how her eyes sparkled whenever she gazed upon him, had Adanya fully realized that the woman's cries had been ones of pleasure.

After that, Adanya had sought out further opportunities to witness this most strange yet provocative act between a man and woman. Her second time, she'd had to climb into tree to view into the brothel window. With the rain beginning to fall about her, she had watched as Dominic threw the woman on the bed, watched as the woman giggled and pretended to wrest away from him. And despite the cool of the raindrops soaking into her clothes, Adanya felt the heat permeate through her loins.

Her third witness occurred in a brothel in Kingston. Dominic had had the company of *two* women then. Adanya had been astounded and mesmerized as always.

One of the women had sat herself upon his face. Peering through the slightly open door, Adanya had reached for the dagger at her hip, thinking she might have to come to his rescue, but it was soon apparent that his life was not in peril.

"I can find a wench for your own," the keeper of the brothel had said to her with a smirk.

Adanya had stared at the woman.

"Suit yourself," the madame had replied, "but me girls are the finest to be had in all of Jamaica."

They had seemed pretty, with their long soft tresses and pale complexions. Looking back into the room, Adanya had battled to keep the aggravation swirling inside her at bay.

But now it was her turn to experience the rapture.

Chapter Four

Miss Wrenwood nestled beside him, her head coming to rest against his chest as she closed her eyes in possible slumber. Dominic lay in bed, staring at the ceiling, unable to keep his thoughts from venturing into the past. Miss Wrenwood had satisfied the momentary tension in his cock, but a deeper yearning remained. As lovely as her cunnie was, it could not compare to Adanya.

He remembered that first moment well. Quite well, to his surprise. The look of wonder upon her face had been nothing short of enchanting. He had no preference for virgins, but somehow it was different with Adanya. He doubted that she knew what her body was capable of. Wondered that she even knew what nature had intended. But she was not one to shun that which she did not understand.

When she threaded her fingers through his hair and pulled his head down, pressing his lips harder to hers, desire lanced surprisingly quick through him. He allowed his weight to sink further onto her. He rolled his hips as he continued to taste of her mouth and marveled at the thickness of her lips. There was so much of her mouth to partake of.

She gasped when he thrust his tongue inside. Her mouth was hot and wet. It did not take her long to respond. Her fingers tightened in his hair, and her hips moved against him. He needed no further encouragement, but reminded himself that this was her first time, perhaps her first kiss.

Though a small part of him still hesitated, still urged him to withdraw, for Adanya was his *crew*, he was a man, and his sex responded to hers in ways that no amount of fortitude could overcome.

After tasting of her mouth fully and at such a length as to

leave her breathless, he kissed his way down her neck to the swell of her bosom. He could taste the faint saltiness of the sea air upon her. He would have liked to avail himself of her swollen orbs, but unpinning her gown and unlacing her stays would cause too much delay and permit him to come to his senses.

His ardor pulsed in his groin. She clung to him as if she might never let him go, her boots pressing heavily into him. She started when he cupped a buttock. How deliciously smooth and toned this part of her flesh was! With a greedy grasp, he held as much of the cheek as he could. Her eyes were wide, but they would grow wider still, for he next moved his hand beneath her leg to the seat of her womanhood. He raised his hips off of her to allow his hand better passage between them.

Settling his hand over her mound, he dipped a thumb to the folds beneath.

Heat flared through him when he found her wet.

If she had been a strumpet, he would have unbuttoned his breeches then. Instead, he gently and languidly brushed his thumb over her. She quivered and a whimper escaped her lips. He had never heard her whimper before. Even as a child, if she had hurt herself, she would do her best to swallow her tears. Being of the weaker sex, she exerted twice the effort of any man. For this reason, Dominic had kept her aboard the *Phantom* long after Mbwana had passed.

His thumb grazed the nub of flesh between her folds. Her mouth dropped, and she looked as if she had been struck by grapeshot. He stroked this most delightful ally till he discovered the manner and spot that produced the greatest gasps. Her wetness grew, and when his ministrations intensified, she began to writhe beneath him. She murmured words he did not recognize, though, upon joining their crew, her father had discouraged the use of their native language.

"The *Phantom* is our home now," Dominic had heard Mbwana tell his daughter.

"Shite!"

That was a word Dominic did know, and Adanya, her brow furrowed, had gasped it as his thumb rubbed her clitoris harder. She struggled beneath him as if she meant to escape, but her grasp upon him tightened.

"Damn me," she murmured between short breaths.

He quickened his fondling. Her lashes fluttered rapidly. Her body tensed.

Softly, he advised, "Do not resist the rapture."

She looked helpless, but within minutes, she was thrown into the sea of carnal bliss. She cried out as the waves crashed over her, sending her body into paroxysm, bumping into him, coaxing his cock to further harden. He eased his caresses, and when the tide had receded for her, she lay with her eyes closed, a flush upon her cheeks, breathing deeply. She had never looked more beautiful.

He could have ended then. Ought to have ended then. He attempted to ignore the painful tension in his crotch. He had not expected that being with Adanya would arouse him to such a degree.

"Is that all?"

He blinked in disbelief at her question. Had she not spent in satisfaction just now?

She pursed her plump lips at him as if he had denied her fair share of rum. "I want a proper fuck."

Bloody hell. Bloody fucking *hell.*

Miss Wrenwood stirred when he took a deep breath. His journey through the past not yet complete, he hoped she would not wake. Despite the pain of recollecting his time with Adanya, he wanted some solitude with his memories.

He saw in her, a captain and pirate in her own right, as much a menace upon the seas as Bartholomew Roberts, the same Adanya he had always known. A woman of defiance. She wanted him and the others to believe that she could be as heartless and fearless as any knave, but Dominic had seen all her aspects.

The hardest moment was when they had lost Mbwana. A raid on an English frigate off the shores of Barbados had gone terribly wrong. Unbeknownst to them, a warship had been laying in hiding on the other side of the cove. A good number of the *Phantom* crew had already boarded the frigate, whose captain had just surrendered, when the warship rounded the bend and began firing scattershot. Dominic called for a retreat as the warship continued its cannon fire. Mbwana had made it back to the *Phantom* but crumbled to the deck beneath a rain of nails and shards of glass.

Dominic crossed onto his own ship and ran to Mbwana. The bloody mangle of flesh was an ominous sight. But Ali brought worse news.

"Adanya," he said.

"What of her?" Dominic asked with a sinking feeling.

"She's not aboard the *Phantom*."

Without pausing to curse, Dominic rushed to the starboard, which was still managing to disengage from its intended quarry, and leaped onto the frigate. He heard Ali following behind him.

"There!" Ali yelled, pointing to where Adanya was fighting off a soldier wielding a bayonet. Taking aim, Dominic shot the redcoat with his pistol.

"Dropped m' flintlock," she huffed, bending down for hers.

By the lack of panic in her demeanor, he gathered she had not seen Mbwana fall. He picked her up, threw her over his shoulder and made his way back aboard the *Phantom*. Before he could set her down, however, she glimpsed her father. With a cry, she attempted to wrest herself from him, but Dominic kept his hold on her and dragged her down into a storeroom in the galley.

"Let me go!" she roared, kicking and clawing at him.

He did so, but only after he had closed the door behind him. She tried to push past him, but he shoved her back.

"Stay here," he told her.

She stared at him, eyes blazing, before dealing a fist to the side of his face. He bit back an oath and grabbed her about the waist before she could pass him. She gave a wild shriek. But he was determined not to let her see her father in his current state.

Scrambling from Dominic, she found her pistol, cocked it and aimed for the center of his chest. "Let me pass."

He squared his shoulders, though by the desperation in her

eyes, he did not doubt her capable of shooting him. Her hands shook so violently, the pistol might go off by accident.

"You'll have to shoot me first," he replied more calmly than he felt.

They stood in silence, regarding one another. He heard Ali above deck, shouting orders to the crew. The *Phantom* gave a welcome groan and began to move.

"Well?" Dominic demanded.

She knit her brows angrily. He could see her making a concerted effort to pull the trigger. Damnation. She *was* going to shoot him. But he stood his ground.

The pistol fired.

Dominic felt the shot reverberate through his body. However, the burn of steel burrowing into flesh did not follow. The bullet had lodged itself into the paneling behind him.

Grabbing the pistol by its barrel, he yanked the firearm from her. He could not know if she had intended to shoot him and merely missed, but it mattered not at present. Her eyes were wide. Her whole body quivered. She looked as if she might cry.

"I will come fetch you," he said softly before departing, taking her pistol with him.

After leaving Adanya locked in the galley, Dominic ascertained the status of the ship. Fortunately, the canon fire from the warship had missed most of its target. The warship did not appear to be attempting pursuit, and the *Phantom* was now out of range of her guns.

Dominic then made straight for Mbwana, who was being tended to by the ship's surgeon on deck. He had Mbwana brought into the captain's quarters and into his own bed. The ship's surgeon cleansed and wrapped the wounds as best he could, but he could not stem the bleeding. When Mbwana was more presentable, Dominic sent for Adanya.

"Take care of her," Mbwana bid Dominic.

He need not have asked. Dominic would have done all he could to honor Mbwana's wishes.

But it was Adanya who had refused to comply.

"Don't want your bloody money," she had said, tossing the purse of gold coins back at him. The sum amounted to a good thousand pounds and would have seen her well settled. Dominic had told her he could arrange for one of the families he knew near Dominica to take her in. She could spend her days strolling the beach, fishing, and eating coconut cakes to her heart's content.

"Then what do you mean to do?" he had demanded after catching the purse of coins.

"The *Phantom* is my home. Don't want to live elsewhere."

"If you stay with us, you're likely to meet the same fate as your father."

She stared at him, stone-faced. He had not meant to speak so harshly, and so soon after Mbwana's death, but gentle words would have been fruitless in the face of her defiance.

"So be it," she had said before turning on her heels.

"I've not dismissed you yet."

She turned back around. He stood up and placed the purse in her hand. "Your father would've wished it."

"But I do not. Now, if you not mind, Captain, I've to clean the lower deck."

She put the coins on his writing table. He could hardly believe it.

"There be a thousand quid worth there," he said. "You're choosing to swab shite and bilge water instead?"

"'Tis my turn," she answered without blinking.

Dominic knew no one more stubborn. She had always possessed an amazing strength of will. It exceeded that of even Mbwana. For certain, it exceeded his own.

* * * * *

In a new set of clothes, with food and drink in her stomach, and an application of Mr. Robbins' poultice, Adanya felt human again.

Sitting on the cot, she thought of the *Sea Falcon* and what she was to do. How soon could she get herself off the *Phantom* and away from Dominic? Should she ask him to take her to nearest land? But few places were safe for pirates nowadays. Should she request they make for Tortuga? Dare she have him sail for where the *Sea Falcon*, if she had escaped, would make berth to tend to her wounds?

Then, to her chagrin, she next wondered if and how often Dominic might have thought of her during their years apart. Undoubtedly, he did not think of her as often she had of him. He had made plain how he had regarded that night when she had truly discovered her womanhood. To him, it had been another tumble in the sack.

She did not fault him for his lack of consideration. She had not intended for that night to hold much significance for her either. She had merely posed a question, and he had answered it. Only it wasn't as simple as asking him to demonstrate the tying of a knot or the aiming of a musket. While it was true she could have asked any member of the crew to take her maidenhead, and she had considered approaching Ali with her request, she had always known it would be Dominic, and could only be Dominic.

He had caused something extraordinary to occur in her body, and the effect of it, alas, had penetrated into her heart. Perhaps if he had merely fucked her then sent her on her way, that night would have held much less sentimentality. She had later come to learn that not all men took the time to see the woman spend. But Dominic had done that and more.

As he had warned, there had been pain. Though he had eased his shaft into her as gently as he could, the breaching of her hymen made her feel as if her body might tear itself in twain. She remembered doing her best to pretend that all was well, but he seemed to know the truth. He stilled, his body propped above hers, brushing soft kisses over her brow. Moments before, his fingers had aroused her with the most tantalizing strokes. Desire overpowered the pain, and when she was ready, he slid himself farther into her.

She looked up at him to see him staring into the depths of her eyes. Had she fallen in love with him at that moment? Or had she always loved him without knowing it?

Delicious sensations rippled from where his groin met hers. The pain receded, replaced by an urge. Slowly, he began to roll his hips into her. She met his thrusts. Before long, she wanted him deeper inside of her, wanted him to fill every inch of her with his hardness. Their bucking caused the bed to thump loudly against the wall, but her cries rose above the noise.

He clamped a hand over her mouth to contain her. It would not do for the crew to hear. There were no other women aboard, and they would know it was her.

As she writhed and slammed against him, she cared not who knew. She finally understood why the men looked forward to the brothels, understood why the women batted their lashes at Dominic. The most wondrous sensations permeated the whole of her being. There was no enchantment to match it. And when the pinnacle of the euphoria swept through her, ravaging her with the force of a hurricane, sending her down into a whirlpool of spasms, she thought she had imploded and wondered that her body would be made whole again.

After several vigorous thrusts, Dominic spent, too. He had muffled her grunts and cries, but his roar could have been easily heard through the doors. He pulled out of her, and wetness hit her inner thigh. He grabbed his cock as more of his mettle spurted from the tip. When his paroxysm appeared to have eased, he collapsed beside her, his breath haggard, his body glistening from perspiration. She, too, felt humid, in part from the exertion but also from the trappings of the gown and stays.

Looking over at him, she saw that he had closed his eyes. She could have left him then. She should have left then. He had satisfied her curiosity beyond measure, in a manner she knew she would never forget.

But she didn't leave. As she pondered what she should say or do or if she should even wonder what the whores he had lain with would do next, she allowed herself to drift to sleep.

She woke to find herself in the crook of his arm, her own arm draped over his midsection, her head upon his chest. Not able to crane her neck to see if he was awake or asleep, she dared not stir. She ought to have asked his permission and not assumed she could remain in his bed.

"How fare you?" he asked.

Relieved he was not cross, she let out the breath she had

been holding. "Well."

"Was it pleasurable for you?"

She fingered the chain of a gold necklace he wore. "Aye, Captain...thank ye, Captain."

In the silence that followed, she savored the closeness of their bodies and how she could feel the rise and fall of his chest as he breathed. At the end of the chain was a large golden coin. It had inscriptions unlike any she had seen before.

"What manner of coin be this?" she asked.

"One I had especially made."

She studied the strange forms engraved onto the surface. "I've seen this coin before. Ali possesses one similar."

"Its mate, a near replica." He held the coin with her. "Not long after Ali and I came to the West Indies, we decided to steal a galleon bound for Mexico. Most of her crew was still on land wenching and drinking. We set a fire on the ship, and the rest of the crew dove into the water as we sailed away. The galleon had the unexpected booty of some four hundred doubloons upon her. As we did not need but a fraction of the treasure, we buried the rest on this island."

Now she understood the shapes on the coin to be a map.

"And what are these markings?" she asked of the lines.

"Chinese numbers denoting the latitude. Ali's coin bears the longitude."

"Chinese?" she asked, impressed. Dominic was unlike any pirate she had heard of.

"Bloody difficult language to learn," he reflected. "Everything about China was bloody difficult."

She tried to imagine what it would have been like to travel on the other side of the world, sailing an entirely different ocean.

"I thought you from Saint Barthélemy. What took you to China?"

"After my mother died, I went in search of my father."

"He was in China?"

"My mother said he was a pirate by the name of Ghandu Bold. She had been aboard a French East India ship returning to France, where she was to wed the son of a merchant. The ship was attacked by Ghandu, and she raped by him. No one would have her then, so she was sent to Saint Barthélemy to live with relations and raise her bastard."

Adanya drew in a breath. Dominic.

"Ghandu had ruined her and sent her to an early death. I went in search of him to kill him."

"Did you find him then?"

"By the most extraordinary of circumstances. He was still sailing the South China Sea and still a pirate."

"And did you kill him?"

"I tried. But, unlike most of the Chinamen I came across, Ghandu was large. He was of Mongol descent. My knife made but a flesh wound in him. I thought for certain he would slice my head off then. I never knew what stayed his hand, but he decided he would punish me by making me work aboard his ship."

"Is that when you turned pirate?"

Dominic nodded.

"Did you try to kill him again?"

"I did. My attempts only amused him. I suspect he knew somehow we were kin, for I had seen him kill others for far less. He started to instruct me in the ways of a pirate and the ways of a man. He taught me how to take a vessel with the least amount of loss, how to earn the respect and loyalty of the crew."

She shifted so that she could see his countenance. "The ways of a man?"

A half grin tugged a corner of his lips. "The first time he let me lay with a whore—it was in Shanghai—he laughed when I was done. Said a child could last longer than I had. The following day, he dragged me into a *jiyuan* and installed me under the tutelage of the aging brothel madam."

"Did you have to lay with her?"

"Aye, and it was by no means pleasurable. But I learned a lot from the old hag. And, since I could not kill him, I wanted to best my father in every way. Ghandu wore jade rings about his cock to lengthen and strengthen his member. He could fuck strumpet after strumpet without tiring."

"And did you best him with the wenches?"

"I stopped trying when he died. Till his final days, I still had thoughts of killing him. But Mei Shan, one of the whores he favored, did what I could not. Drove a sword straight into his heart as he slept in her bed. She was later killed by his crew. By then, I had had my fill of the China seas and began to make my way back to Saint Barthélemy."

"You kept his name."

"Aye, I took his name. My real name be Dominic Laurel, but I have no loyalty to the name of Laurel. My mother was treated poorly by her family. I suppose I paid Ghandu some regard. He was a fine pirate."

As are you, she wanted to say.

Chapter Five

Disengaging from Miss Wrenwood while she slept, Dominic replaced the fall of his breeches and, easing into his coat, strode out onto the quarterdeck. The wind blowing through his hair would have filled the square sails well, but the *Phantom* was heaving to, awaiting direction from him as to where she should head.

He expected Adanya would want to find her ship, and he intended to ask her where the *Sea Falcon* would likely make berth. But he was reluctant to relinquish her so soon. He had never thought to see her again and half expected that whenever he heard her name, it would be to learn of her death. He hoped, in that event, that she had died by sword or gunshot. He feared her capture by the British, and would sooner have killed her himself than let her fall into their hands. She had taken far too many of their slave ships for them to grant her any leniency.

The stories her victims told painted her a vicious savage who drank the blood of her dead, a wild and ruthless barbarian without the grace of reason or intelligence. That she was a blackamoor and a woman only made her more incomprehensible, and it was supposed that she must have been possessed by the worst of demons.

Dominic doubted she was as bloodthirsty as claimed, though he had taught her that a pirate must first instill fear. It was their greatest weapon.

He remembered the first time she had killed. He had been reluctant to permit her any participation in the raids, but after five and some years of sailing aboard the *Phantom*, Mbwana had said it was time. They attacked a merchant ship sailing from Antigua. They boarded the ship with their usual show of wildness and chants of "Death! Death! Death!" Adanya had been excited to take part.

The merchantman's crew had armed themselves, but their resistance had not lasted long. After surrendering, the shipmaster and his sailors were made to sit on the deck while the crew from the *Phantom* began relieving the ship of its cargo.

Adanya had recognized one of the sailors and lunged at him. Dominic later learned that the sailor had served aboard the *Bountiful* and raped many of the slave women, including a girl not twelve years of age who was a cousin to Adanya.

Before anyone could restrain the sailor, he had clocked Adanya over the head. She had whipped out her dagger and drove the blade into his throat. He had fallen to the deck, clutching the dagger. Adanya had begun kicking his convulsing body.

No one had stopped her until Dominic ordered Ali to take her back to the *Phantom*. Dominic had later found her at the ship's head, hurling from the seat of easement to the waters below. She had remained sick for several days after, requiring a bucket next to her bunk at every hour.

Dominic inhaled the salty, moist air and cursed. Perhaps he would have been more fortunate had their paths never again crossed. After she had deserted him—and taken Ali with her—he had not gone in pursuit. It would have been fruitless. There was no man more skilled at evading capture than Ali. But if they were done with him, then he was done with them.

Though Ali had pledged his life to Dominic, who had discovered him marooned on an island in the Arabian Sea, it was Adanya's desertion that rankled him more. He had made a place for her aboard the *Phantom*, had granted her opportunities that no captain ought to have granted a woman, and this was how she had repaid him—by stealing his first mate and his gold?

Allowing her onto his ship had been a grand mistake. But perhaps the greater had been in lying with her. He had deluded himself into thinking all would remain the same thereafter.

"This'll not happen again," he had told her after wiping the blood, the evidence of her breached maidenhead, from her inner thigh.

He watched her pull on her boots and push the gown down her legs as she rose from his bed. He would have liked another glimpse of her shapely legs. He had never caressed such smoothness. Her kind had very little hair upon the limbs.

"Yours is the first watch following breakfast, eh?" he inquired.

"Aye, Captain."

"You had best change then."

"Happily," she replied. "Don't fathom why women would wish to wear such uncomfortable garments."

He was relieved that she did not seem to wish to tarry as the women he bedded often wanted, but Adanya did pause at the threshold. She turned only her head to the side.

"Thank ye, Captain," she said, as if he had merely granted her another ration of rum. She left before he could make a response.

Adanya was not like others of her sex, Dominic assured himself, to temper the regret he was starting to feel. She swabbed the ship's head, raised and lowered the yards, slaughtered the livestock, and manned the pumps with less complaint than most men in his crew. She even wielded a cutlass and pistol as well as any. He expected she would not approach him again.

But he was wrong. And wrong to think he could withstand the temptation that was Adanya.

She had allowed him into her breeches twice more. Each time was finer than the last. But he knew he had to put a stop to their trysts. The crew would come to know of it, and he would be seen as a hypocrite. Once, a drunken crewman had grabbed Adanya, wanting a kiss. Dominic had sentenced the man to be flogged around the fleet. Dominic had then threatened to set the hairs of their groin on fire if a man dared make mischief with Adanya.

To convince himself that he would no longer crave her body, he had tumbled as many whores as he could each time they came into port. He had stayed away from Adanya.

But now, with her back on his ship, he could not ignore her or the sentiments he had thought buried too deep in his bosom to see the light of day. Could he forgive her the past?

* * * * *

Unable to take her mind off Dominic and finding the confines of the cabin stifling, Adanya decided to walk the ship.

She went about and greeted the familiar faces among the *Phantom's* crew, somewhat expecting to begin old friendships where they had left off. But while the men greeted her with nods, it became clear that she was no longer the Adanya who would steal biscuits from them as a little girl or the fellow crew member who sang bawdy songs as badly out of tune as they did. Instead, she was Captain Mbwana, a stranger. Only Mr. Withers, now with strands of grey streaking his beard, regarded her without the gulf forged by five years of absence.

"Me arse, but if it ain't little Ya-Ya," Mr. Withers said, throwing a gruff arm about her shoulders and smashing her into his ample chest.

"A little too much breadfruit and rum of late?" Adanya asked, indicating his rounded belly after he had released her.

"Our latest pillage has turned up as much victuals as gold," Mr. Withers admitted. "No sense in lettin' it go to waste."

He looked her over. "Ye grown prettier since I saw you last. Cap'n Mbwana, is it? Yer father woulda been proud."

Adanya sat down on top of a barrel of ale. Every time she raided a slave ship, she thought of her father. He had never said specifically why he chose to join the *Phantom* instead of returning home with the other slaves, but she knew that she lived the destiny he had aspired to for himself.

"Cap'n Bold, too," Mr. Withers added.

"Eh?"

"Cap'n Bold—he be mighty proud as well, though he cursed you through and through the day you left."

"He curses me still," Adanya said.

Withers shrugged. "But he was fair burstin' his stitches when he heard the bounty the English set on your head. Said you set free some thousands of slaves."

Adanya had stopped counting, for she had raided ships that carried as many as eight hundred slaves at a time. It disconcerted her that she was less interested in what Withers had to say about her achievements than his insights into what Dominic thought. Dominic had introduced her with flourishing words, but she yearned to know what he really felt.

Only it was senseless to care what he thought. She wasn't about to do anything different based on the sentiments of one man. A man she hadn't seen in five years. And whom she would be relieved not to have to see for another five years.

Supper proved uncomfortable enough. Miss Wrenwood, sitting to Dominic's left, had flushed cheeks, her hair in slight disarray, her gown wrinkled. Adanya had no doubt that Miss Wrenwood had recently lifted her skirts beneath Dominic, and since she could not wholly blame Miss Wrenwood for wanting to lay with the captain, she directed her unsavory feelings at *him* while shocking Miss Wrenwood with tales of her exploits. Storytelling was in her blood, and Adanya had everyone at the table entranced.

"A terrible abomination," Mr. Robbins said of slavery after Adanya had recounted how she had attacked one slave ship that had been in the midst of tossing its slaves overboard in order to collect on the insurance of its "cargo."

"But Father says these slaves are savage beings," Miss Wrenwood offered, "and that we provide a path to salvation they otherwise would not have."

"That the English profit from them makes it all a greater blessing," said Dominic wryly as he pushed himself back from the table and propped one ankle over the knee of his other leg.

"The English are not the only ones with slave ships."

"But none can rival the English in volume and profit in that trade."

"I have seen babes torn from their mothers' tits," said Adanya, "and tossed crying into the sea. Children hung to die to punish their mothers and fathers. Where is the salvation in the deaths of children?"

"Are you suggesting there is honor to your piracy?" Miss

Wrenwood challenged.

Dominic lifted his mug of ale. "To a pirate's honor. Our souls are damned, but I believe a greater hell exists for those in the slave trade."

"Here, here," said Robbins, lifting his glass.

Adanya felt her heart swell as she looked at Dominic. In many ways, he was the oddest pirate she had ever known, but she would have him no other way.

"But where is the fortune in attacking slave ships if you only mean to set the slaves free?" Rowland asked.

"We pillage our fair share of other merchant ships," Adanya answered.

"And a booty of a few hundred doubloons to start does no harm," Dominic voiced.

Adanya glanced sharply at him, but before she could respond, Miss Wrenwood made a comment about how much she missed having sweetmeats after supper. She continued to talk of matters that Adanya found tedious. The manner in which Miss Wrenwood cast glances beneath her lashes at Dominic and the way her lips turned up demurely at the corners was an art that Adanya was familiar with, having seen many other women perform the same before Dominic, but one that she knew she could never accomplish.

Seated next to Rowland, Adanya could feel the man's gaze upon her numerous times. She could sense his desire the way a prey could sometimes sense its predator. For a fleeting moment, she entertained the idea of bedding the first mate. It had been years since she had had a tumble in the sack with anyone. She spent her days at sea surrounded by men, and she had not been above a few daydreams regarding some in her crew. But she never risked it. Her brief dalliance with Dominic had shown her how quickly a friendship could deteriorate.

After supper, in the solitude of her cabin, sitting on the narrow bed in the corner of the room, with only the faint light of moon for illumination, she inched her hand down her breeches to find her mons. Being so close to Dominic was maddening. She imagined Dominic's hard, muscular body over the soft, supple body of Miss Wrenwood. Her own body warmed at the thought, even as she tried to cast out the hurtful image. Her fingers slid along her folds. She leaned her head against the wall and closed her eyes, remembering what it felt like to feel herself pressed against him.

A sound outside the door prompted her to whip out her hand and grab the dagger from her thigh strap. She leaped to her feet and waited behind the door. When it opened, she pounced, intending to hold her dagger to the man's throat.

But this time he was ready for her. He grabbed her arm, twisting it and the dagger behind her back. Her face and body were shoved against the wall next to the door.

"I want my gold back, Adanya," said Dominic.

Chapter Six

Adanya cringed, not from the pain of being pressed against the wall, but from a hurt deep within. That was what Dominic cared about. His damn doubloons. Indignation flared, and she attempted to throw him off her, but he held fast. As strong as she was, he had more than twice her strength. She dropped her dagger. It clattered to the floor between them.

"If you've not noticed, I haven't so much as a piece upon me," Adanya said.

Dominic released her. Rubbing her wrist, Adanya turned to glare at him through the semi-darkness.

"Where's the gold?" Dominic demanded.

"I might give ye an answer, if you ask nice, like."

He shot his arm out towards the wall, his palm landing inches from her ear. "That don't be something a pirate would know."

Her heart hammered against her sides. The proximity of his body to hers made her painfully aware of how much larger he was and how easily he could overpower her. She could smell his essence mixed with the stench of ale. There was a blaze in his eyes that she had never seen before, and it frightened her.

Slipping away from him, she said with disgust, "You've been drinking."

"Not nearly enough," he responded.

Adanya glanced at her dagger on the floor. He saw her eye movement and placed his boot on top of the dagger.

"It isn't enough for you to steal my gold and run off with m' first mate, but you would cut me, too?"

She wanted to scream at him that she never took his gold, never took so much as a reale from him. But she didn't. It wouldn't have done any good. He had obviously convinced himself that she was the culprit. And it hurt. It hurt something fierce that he would think that of her.

"What need have you of those old doubloons for?" Adanya said instead. "Surely Miss Wrenwood can fetch a fair sum for you?"

"Not two hundred doubloons' worth."

"Then you've caught yourself the wrong wrench," replied Adanya with an indifferent shrug that belied her true feelings. She needed to escape from Dominic, but he stood not two feet in front of the door. "Though I suppose she's good for a fuck."

Hell, why had she gone and said that? She certainly didn't want Dominic to think that she was jealous in any way.

"Shouldn't you be attending to her?" Adanya added with raised eyebrows.

"When I have done with you."

Adanya bristled under his stare. The thought of him sliding into bed with Miss Wrenwood riled her. She would be but an afterthought as he buried himself in Miss Wrenwood's cunt.

Desperate now to rid herself of his presence, Adanya replied with clenched hands, "You think I wouldn't have spent your bloody doubloons by now?"

A muscle rippled along his jaw. "All of it?"

"All of it."

She was certain he had had a fair amount to drink, but his hand shot towards her and gripped her throat with startling accuracy. His thumb and fingers encircled her neck. He nearly lifted her to her toes.

"I ought to throw you to the English and collect the bounty on your head."

Adanya gripped his forearm with both of her hands, though if he decided to strangle her, there was naught she could do.

"Aye," Adanya grunted defiantly, "you'd be a fool not to."

Dominic pressed his lips into a grim line. His hand tightened about her throat. He pulled her head towards him and crushed her mouth to his.

Adanya nearly cried out at the pain, but all she could manage was a muffle against his bruising lips. She struggled to separate herself, feeling as if her lips would be melded to her teeth with the pressure. With his mouth, he sucked the air from her, drowning her in his kiss.

Head reeling, she thought about bringing her knee to his groin. How dare he take such liberties after accusing her of something that would have had them drawing swords at dawn? How dare he when he had no doubt come from being with Miss Wrenwood? How dare he...

But as his mouth opened to clamp down farther upon hers, Adanya felt her resistance ebbing, weak against the tide of more powerful emotions. Her lips parted underneath his and she returned his kiss every bit as fiercely.

* * * * *

Dominic felt a surge of heady triumph when he felt Adanya succumb to him, though in his current state of wrath and longing, he was quite likely to proceed with or without her assent. He could feel the ale tampering with his mind, but most of all, he felt desire. Desire that had been pent up for five years, and there was little that Adanya needed to do to set it free.

He had gone at Miss Wrenwood after having seen Adanya naked before Mr. Robbins, but his release had brought no satisfaction. Instead, his cock had risen again upon seeing Adanya at supper. The breeches and shirt she wore molded to her body. She had not bound her chest, her breasts heavy like melons ripe for picking. His hands itched to do the harvesting of those beautiful globes.

Plundering her mouth with his own, their tongues dueling for position, Dominic felt his cock strain painfully against his clothes, his cods a boiling cauldron of raw animal lust. When she shoved her tongue towards the back of his throat, he knew there was no containing the beast. There would be no tender foreplay, no patient caresses. Only a mad desire to claim her. To avenge himself for all the pain she had caused.

To banish any man she had ever lain with and to prove to her that she was his.

Grabbing her shirt, he wrenched it down past her shoulders

and seared her throat and collarbone with his mouth. Her skin was warm and faintly salty. He circled his arm around her, lifting her, and spun around to pin her back against the wall. He pulled open the front of her shirt. She had the largest and most beautiful areolas. He devoured her breasts with his mouth. She wrapped her legs around him and wound her fingers through his hair, locking his head against her.

Unable to extricate her breeches whilst her legs were wrapped around him, he grabbed the waist and ripped the pants along the crotch. He reached a hungry hand between her thighs. When he found her sopping wet, he nearly lost his mind. He claimed her mouth once more as he pushed fingers up her quim. She gasped, then groaned. Her cunnie strained and grasped at his fingers.

Dominic used his free hand to loosen his own breeches. His cock sprang forth as if desperate for air. His entire groin was on fire. It sought the relief of her wetness. He grabbed her thighs and, without ceremony, shoved his shaft into her waiting sheath.

Her cunnie was a furnace. He could have succumbed instantly. She deserved no more. But he needed her to spend. To have her body surrender in delight.

He allowed her to grind her pelvis against him. Groaning, she lifted his head and crushed her lips to his. In her passion, she bit him several times, hard. He responded by thrusting his hips into her. The small cabin filled with the sound of his body slapping into hers, of her slamming against the wall, of their grunting and labored breathing. And then her cries of ecstasy. A melodious sound.

She shook violently in his arms and would have fallen to the floor if he did not hold her aloft. He pushed his cock farther into her quim and roared with his own release. Despite having spent twice that day already, and with the effect of the ale still in him, the climax was a whirlpool, sucking him into rapture and overwhelming him with more than ecstasy.

When the shuddering climax dissipated, he found himself still gasping for air. Fearing he might have pounded into her too forcefully, he carried her over to her cot and gently laid her down. Through the pain and anger, he tenderly kissed her underneath her jaw, the dip at the base of her throat, the top of her breasts.

He lay down beside her, and she did not push him away. He could do so much for her. Hold her. Protect her. Satisfy her. He wanted to say as much, but he feared shattering the moment by speaking. Instead, the words lay lodged in his throat. He could have conveyed his thoughts through his eyes, but she lay with her eyes closed, still recovering.

His hand skimmed her thigh. She would need new breeches. He fingered the torn opening of the crotch, wet with their desires, then slid his finger into her cunnie. It was as tight as Miss Wrenwood's, but unlike Miss Wrenwood, and even the many whores that he had bedded, Adanya possessed a strong body and was unafraid to use it. No woman ground herself into him as she did. No quim flexed against his cock as ravenously.

When he pulled out his finger and stroked the nub of flesh between her folds, she sighed. He continued to stroke her, occasionally dipping his finger into the reservoir of wetness between her thighs. She shifted her hips and parted her legs a little wider. He lowered his head over one breast and suckled it. His cock stirred to life again.

Was it true that absence made the heart fonder? Or was it the way she carried herself as Captain Mbwana that made him crave her more than ever? He had deluded himself into thinking that fucking her once would be enough to dispel the demons. He wanted her again.

Adanya panted with his caresses. He quickened his strokes and gave her what she wanted, pushing her over the edge until she trembled with spasms.

His cock as hard as the mizzenmast, Dominic rolled on top of her and pushed himself into her. This time his thrusts were long and drawn. Not yet completely over her first climax, Adanya caught the wave of a second. She screamed and gripped his arms painfully. He pistoned in and out of her to bring about his own release. It wasn't as intense as the one he had experienced but moments before, but he collapsed atop her nonetheless.

After a moment to collect himself, Dominic lifted his weight off her and looked into her face. Little beads of perspiration dotted the tip of her nose. Her thick black eyelashes rested against her cheeks. Her even breathing indicated that she had fallen asleep. He realized she needed the rest badly.

After pulling up his breeches, he removed her boots and stockings for her and pulled a blanket over her.

Before returning to his own quarters, he stopped upon the threshold to study the tranquility upon her face. In this state of peace, her guard down, she was not Captain Mbwana, but Adanya. The Adanya he remembered.

After five long years, she was back in his life, and he wasn't about to let her slip away. She belonged with him. But how to make the proud and indomitable Captain Mbwana his?

Chapter Seven

Adanya awoke with a start, expecting to see her own cabin but finding herself in a much smaller space. She was not aboard the *Sea Falcon*. She was on the *Phantom*—Dominic's ship. The soreness between her legs was a reminder of his presence.

She sat up and saw clean linen and a new pair of breeches folded at the foot of the bed then remembered that he had torn the ones she was wearing. She dropped her head to her knees and cursed. Damn her woman's weakness. What must he think of her now? No different than any other woman who simpered and swooned in his arms. Devil take it, she was a pirate captain. Feared and fearsome. Would he now simply see her as a bitch in heat? Perhaps he had always seen her that way.

In disgust, Adanya threw aside the blanket and changed her torn breeches for the new pair. She pulled on her boots and tied a kerchief over her head, trying not to remember the particulars of what had happened between her and Dominic last night. If she dwelled too long upon the memories, she feared her body would begin to yearn again for his.

In search of breakfast, she sought out Mr. Withers, who offered to cook her up some porridge.

"Salt pork and hardtack will do," said Adanya, famished. She had not eaten much supper the night before, her hunger having been eclipsed by the tumultuous feelings related to Dominic.

"What happened to the crew?" she asked after accepting a mug of coffee from Mr. Withers. "More than half the faces are unfamiliar to me."

"We had one right bad raid near Saint Domingue. A French warship came upon us and we lost a number of men in that skirmish."

Despite her anger at Dominic, Adanya felt a pang of shared grief.

"But we also had a good run on sugar," said Mr. Withers. "Made a fair lot selling it to Dutch importers. After that, many of us had the means to retire."

"Why didn't you?"

Withers scratched his thinning hair. "Don't rightly know. S'pose I don't know no other life. I was born a seadog, I'll die a seadog. An' Captain Bold's been good to me."

The man's loyalty touched her, and she regretted that she could not do the same by Dominic.

"Tell me of Rowland. How long has he been first mate?"

"Not long. 'Came highly regarded by the crew after he had slain a dozen men aboard a privateer that attacked us. They said he came upon a man twice his size, yet Rowland broke the scurvy's neck with his own hands."

"He don't seem the sort of man I would have reckoned Dom—Captain Bold to choose as his first mate," Adanya commented as she thought about Rowland and how a sense of danger lurked in the man's ocean-blue eyes.

"Well, you ran off with his best."

Adanya flushed. "Ali deserted me as well. Captain Bold was better off without him."

"Mayhap. But not without you."

Withers was examining the salt provisions, his face turned away from her. Could what he said be possibly true? But as quick as her hopes rose, Adanya dashed them. Withers was softhearted. He did not know the uncomfortable, indeterminate state that she and Dominic had occupied after she had given her virginity to him. They had lain together a few more times after that, careful to hide it from the crew. She had told herself that the nature of her relationship with Dominic had not changed. He was still her captain, and she his pilot.

But that was where her folly had lain. The nature had changed. Or, rather, she had changed. She had come to see Dominic as more than just her captain. Dominic, however, had not seemed to consider her more than his pilot, no different from the rest of the crew save for her cunnie and breasts.

When they had docked in Tortuga, Dominic had gone to visit his usual whorehouse. That was when Adanya realized she could not be but a pilot to Dominic.

She had approached Ali about venturing off on their own. It had been brazen of her to approach Dominic's first mate, a man who had known Dominic years before he had become captain of his own ship. But Ali had been partial to her. She had seen it in his eyes, and though she could not return his affection at the time, she had thought she might. When, two years later, it became apparent to them both that she could not, Ali had left her, in the same manner she had left Dominic, without warning and without word.

The desperation she had felt had changed little. She was still better off putting as much distance between herself and Dominic as possible.

But first she had to get off the *Phantom*.

Adanya decided she would ask Dominic if he would sail first toward St. Kitts. From there she could make her way to the little-known island where the *Sea Falcon* made berth. She thanked Withers for the breakfast and, not seeing Dominic on deck, headed towards his cabin.

She stood in front of his door, unable to knock. Facing a British man-of-war would have taken less courage. At the moment, she would have rather faced the entire fleet of King George than see Dominic after what had happened last night. If he had wanted to make known his anger at her, he had done it in the way he had fucked her. He had then sealed his triumph by bringing her to spend once more. And she had willingly surrendered to his caresses.

No. The ocean of difference between Adanya and Captain Mbwana was vast. Adanya would have nursed her wounds, perhaps indulged in self-pity. Captain Mbwana would surge into battle, enflamed by her wounds. Captain Mbwana had not the luxury to consider anything else.

Adanya knocked on the door soundly. When silence greeted her, she tried the handle, ready to walk in with pronounced steps to demand that the *Phantom* let her off at St. Kitts.

The door opened, but Dominic was not in sight. Instead, she

saw his large four-post bed. Miss Wrenwood, naked, quickly grabbed the bed covers and pulled them over her breasts.

Miss Wrenwood opened her mouth to speak, but Adanya turned around and left before a word was uttered.

Chapter Eight

The strange ache pressing the backs of her eyes felt like tears. Adanya reasoned that she was still weakened from her ordeal of the past few days, faced with the devastating prospect that she may have lost her ship and crew...but the simple answer was that five years had not been enough to bury her feelings for Dominic.

Turning the corner, she walked into something tall and hard.

"Captain Mbwana!" Rowland greeted as he reached out a hand to steady her.

"Mr. Stirling," Adanya responded and looked down at his hand upon her arm.

His lips turned up at one corner as he brazenly looked into her eyes before releasing his hold. "Mr. Robbins was looking for you. Said he had more salve for you. If you would follow me, we can procure the ointment."

Adanya studied the man and decided she believed what Mr. Withers had said of the first mate. Here was a man she was decidedly *not* safe with.

"Very well," Adanya assented and followed Rowland back below deck.

"I take it you know your way abouts this ship," Rowland commented.

As if it were yesterday. But Adanya kept the thought to herself.

"Must have been odd being the only woman aboard the ship," Rowland continued. "Odd that Dominic would have allowed it."

"We'd had any number of Miss Wrenwoods aboard," said Adanya dismissively.

"Not among the crew. Dominic must have considered you...special."

"I was. I was the best pilot that ever steered the *Phantom*."

Rowland shook his head and eyed her appreciatively from head to toe. "Dominic could have trained any number of aspiring mates. He chose you."

Adanya returned his stare. What was he getting at?

"Well, it don't matter none now, do it? I'm Captain of my own ship."

"Ah, yes," Rowland said simply as they stopped in front of his cabin. "Mr. Robbins has left the salve with me."

He opened the door and held it for her. Adanya felt an itch to grab her dagger, but she walked in resolutely. The door closed behind them.

She whipped around as Rowland reached for her and instead of grasping her dagger, she grasped him by his cods.

"Lay a hand on me and I'll make bloody sure you never walk the same again," she threatened.

Rowland grimaced when she squeezed his scrotum. "I can see why Dominic liked you."

She stared at him, then, with a curt laugh, released him and stepped back.

"Nothing like a bit of ebony to go with all the fair cunnies he's had."

She frowned but wasn't about to let him see how much his comment disturbed her. He seemed to guess it nonetheless.

"You fucked him," Rowland threw at her.

"Among many others," she returned.

"Would you consider adding one more to your count?"

This time it was her mouth that turned up at the corner in a half-smile. Perhaps this was what she needed—another tumble to drive out all thoughts of Dominic.

Sensing her hesitation, Rowland approached her. When he reached for her, she did not stop him. With both hands, he gripped her shoulders and brought his mouth to hers. His lips were thinner. He tasted different. Smelled different.

It wasn't going to work, she realized. She would simply be spending the entire time comparing him to Dominic, and he would be found wanting.

"Well, well. It seems you're getting quite the welcome aboard my ship, Captain Mbwana."

Adanya jumped away from Rowland. From the doorway, Dominic gazed at them with little fires in his eyes.

"Captain Bold...we...I..." Rowland fumbled for words.

"See that Mr. Collins has made an accurate count of the rations."

"But I have already seen to—"

"See to it again, Mr. Stirling."

Rowland pressed his lips together in displeasure, but he answered, "Aye, Captain," before leaving.

Adanya went to follow, but Dominic stopped her. He narrowed his eyes at her.

"Planning to seduce another one of my first mates into deserting me?" he inquired.

"Damn you," she said as she threw aside his arm, but he grabbed her and pulled her into his body. The memory of how forcefully he had taken her last night, the feel of his hard body pressed to her, warmed her loins in an instant.

"I'll be damned if I let you fuck one of my crew," Dominic said.

"I'll fuck whomever I please," she replied with equal vigor. "I'm not of your crew to order about anymore."

"Order about? You never took orders well. But by God, captain or no, you'll take this one."

His arrogance infuriated her. His nearness enflamed her.

"Take your bloody hands off me," she spat.

"You seemed quite delighted to have them upon you last night," he returned.

"A moment of weakness," she retorted, "brought about by floatin' in the sea for two days."

"Indeed?" He picked her up by the collar of her shirt and dragged her to the small bed against the wall.

She tried to pull herself free, but he threw her onto the bed. She landed on her back. "Should ye not be with Miss Wrenwood now?" she asked desperately.

"I've no interest in Miss Wrenwood," he said, staring at her with an intensity that made her heart leap. "It's you I want, Captain Mbwana."

His words were nearly her undoing. He took advantage of the pause to advance upon her. She rolled away before he could cover her with his body, but he was as quick as she and stronger. He yanked her back beneath him before she could get her knees between them. She struggled but could not throw him off of her, not with him lying between her legs. His hand went straight between her thighs, rubbing her intimately, until her fist connected with his jaw. He grunted then yanked both her arms above head. With one hand, he circled her slender wrists and kept them pinned to the bed. He shoved his other down the front of her breeches.

"What have we here?" he asked her with a cocked brow, then pulled out his hand, his fingers glistening with her wetness.

"It not be for ye," she lied.

It was the wrong thing to say.

His body tensed as if ready to attack. Though a part of her reveled in the fact that she could make him jealous, she was feeling more afraid than triumphant.

He pressed his lips together grimly before saying, "Rowland and I have shared a few women. They come back to me more than not—as will you."

"You've a haughty notion of yourself."

"I lay you a wager then, Captain Mbwana. If I fail to make you spend, you can fuck any member of my crew and I relinquish my claim to the doubloons you stole."

"I never stole—"

"But if I win, you will repay what you took from me by being mine—mine to take at will, whenever and wherever I wish."

She inhaled sharply. He wanted her as his whore? Captain Mbwana as Captain Bold's wench?

"Not bloody likely," she huffed.

But as he ran his finger along her clit, she shuddered involuntarily. Her body was succumbing to him. It *wanted* to succumb to him. She tried to remain still and ignore all sensation. She envisioned various homely members of her crew: her boatswain, whose face was shaped like a horse, her master rigger with the bulbous nose, a gunner with five missing teeth.

She tried to conjure up all the jealousy and anger she felt towards Dominic. He was an arrogant bleeder. He had accused her of stealing from him. Propositioned her with a bet that she could not walk away from without conceding defeat, but one that she could not afford to lose.

It's you I want.

The words haunted her, and his gentle fondling could not be ignored. His fingers felt too fine against her. She wanted him, wanted his cock inside her once more. Their fucking last night had done nothing to diminish her craving for him.

Grasping what remained of her resistance, she knew she had to do something fast before her body betrayed her completely. Moaning, she ground herself at his hand, her body writhing in wantonness.

She stared him straight in the eyes. "Fuck me."

The flames in his eyes flared. Releasing her wrists, he went to undo the buttons of his fall.

Seizing the moment, she grabbed the dagger from her thigh and laid the blade against the side of his throat.

"You wouldn't," he said, his stare solemn.

"Wouldn't I? You thought me capable of stealing the doubloons you and Ali had hidden. What else might I be capable of?"

"No one knew where the doubloons were. No one but you, and I was a fool to have told you."

"Ali knew where they were."

"Ali would have taken only his share."

Angry that he believed better of Ali than he did of her, she pressed her dagger harder at him. The damned bastard deserved to have his blood drawn.

"Get up," she ordered.

He pushed himself away. She kept the dagger at his throat and pushed his chest, forcing him to lie down upon the bed. She glanced at his crotch, where a bulge still remained.

"Perhaps I will spend, Captain Bold. But on my terms. You

can be *my* wench."

With her free hand, she undid his breeches. His cock sprang free. She eyed it with hunger and felt her cunnie throb. She pulled her own breeches down, baring the lower half of her body. He stared at her limber legs, the swell of her hips, and the patch of black curls that led to her woman's paradise. She straddled him and ground her cunnie at his shaft, her wetness allowing her to glide upon his length with ease.

He moaned when she quickened her motions. The tension pooling in her nether regions began to flare beautifully throughout her body. He grabbed her hips to aid her motions. The pressure in her built till she could bear the emptiness in her cunnie no longer. She speared herself upon him.

With the dagger still at his throat, she fucked him in earnest. He bucked his hips at her.

"You'll not want to spend before I do," she cautioned.

"Not bloody likely," he echoed of her earlier words. "I make you spend first, you're mine."

He spoke with frightening conviction, and she remembered the stories he would tell of Gandhu Bold. Though Dominic did not wear jade rings about his cock, she did not doubt that he acquired more skills in pleasuring a woman than most men would know in a lifetime.

"Afraid to take me on?" Dominic asked.

"And if I win, I'll frig your first mate while you watch."

His eyes blazed in jealousy. She had no intention of lying with Mr. Stirling, but Dominic deserved a bit of torment.

His jaw tightened and he began to roll his hips with deliberation, drawing his cock out slowly, as if to ensure the most perfect angle. Her cunnie clenched about him in response. In this manner, their bodies dueled to see whose forbearance would last.

His grip upon her hips tightened as he lifted her, then eased her down his shaft till the nub at her folds ground against his pelvis. His stratagem was working as waves of pleasure flooded her insides and rippled through her legs. She tried to resist. But for what purpose? Why not submit to the most exquisite rapture her body could know? Why not be his?

The truth was she had overestimated herself. Before yesterday, she had not lain with a man in years. She could not. Not as Captain Mbwana.

He quickened his thrusting, making the pressure inside her build and build. She wanted to spend, wanted that carnal glory. She moved in rhythm with him and relished his grunts and groans. She could see the tide threatening to wash over and held out as long as she could.

But she could not stop it any more than she could hold back the sea. The paroxysm overcame her, shaking her body and drowning her in euphoria. With a roar, Dominic shoved himself into her, hard and deep. She felt a burst of liquid heat inside of her as she continued to tremble and gasp.

Their bodies rolled through spasm after spasm till she collapsed atop his chest. Overcome, she knew not if she had won or lost. For the moment, it mattered not. If she had run up the white flag, it felt wonderful.

* * * * *

"Why did you leave, Adanya?"

She lay beside Dominic, the rhythmic rise and fall of his chest lulling her into a tranquil place. He had an arm encircled about her in a half embrace.

What was she to say? That she loved him too much sounded inane.

"I wished to captain my own ship," Adanya said. It was partially true.

"Why did you not come to me? Why leave without a fare-thee-well?"

A lump crept up her throat. The quietness of his tone was more difficult to handle than if he had spoken harshly.

"I was young. I knew little."

"I knew what your father wished, Adanya. I would have supported you."

Adanya. Not Captain Mbwana. But Adanya. He had spoken her name a few times already. Each time it was like a caress on his lips. It made them sound like lovers.

"You could not. My crew serves me not for riches. What commerce we have is but to sustain our attacks on the slave ships."

"Is that how you received this scar—in an attack?" He traced the thin, uneven line that scratched her cheek.

"The end of a cutlass," Adanya acknowledged. "My second attempt on a slave ship leaving Bance Island."

"And this one?" He ran his knuckles along a short scar on her jaw.

"Took a tumble down the stairs of the poop deck."

Dominic smiled. Her heart surged. All else melted away. The world held but the two of them and time ceased to exist.

Briefly.

"Captain, the rations have been counted."

Rowland had returned. Adanya scrambled to pull up her breeches and strap her dagger on.

"Good," Dominic replied, also rising to his feet.

As if it was quite common for him to bugger women in Rowland's cabin, Dominic strode past the glowering first mate and held the door open for Adanya.

As she and Dominic were about to climb the steps to the deck, Dominic grabbed her around the waist with one arm. With his other hand, he cupped the back of her head and brought his lips to her ear.

"I want you again, Adanya," he murmured, his cock hardening against her leg. "I have matters to discuss with my quartermaster, but come to my cabin in an hour's time."

He took her mouth with his, deeply and passionately, but without the anger of the last kiss. It amazed Adanya how quickly his touch enflamed her loins and caused her wetness to flow.

With steps of air, Adanya walked the deck. The wind blowing by her seemed fresher, full of promise as the ship cut through the ocean waves. She could hardly wait an hour to be with Dominic again. She stopped to admire the *Phantom* in full sail. It was the most beautiful ship to her. She loved the *Sea Falcon*, but it was built for speed. The *Phantom* was more voluptuous.

She turned to seek out Dominic's pilot and query the man on their coordinates, but a pair of rough hands grabbed her from behind.

Chapter Nine

Though Dominic had been confident that he could bring Adanya to spend, it had proven more difficult than expected. While buried in her, he'd had to fight back his own release, which had threatened to shoot from his cock on numerous occasions.

They had enjoyed a peaceful moment together after their vigorous lovemaking. For once, Dominic thought he understood what Buddhist monks hoped to attain. Her body curled next to his, her sweet head on his chest—it was the natural order of things. There were no feelings at war, only the serenity of the seas after a storm. He could have killed Rowland for abbreviating the moment.

He needed her. No other woman had excited such desire, such longing, such bliss, and such lust. His cock hungered for her time and time again. He smiled to himself as he thought of the different ways he would collect upon his wager. He could tie her to his bed, compel her to pleasure his cock with her tongue, have her sit atop his groin. He loved that position. Lithe and nimble, she could ride his cock like no other. And he had full view and access to her heavy, bounding breasts.

"You were with her—that woman pirate," Miss Wrenwood said when Dominic entered his cabin.

How long had she been here, he wondered, taking in her slim, naked legs protruding from beneath his bed covers.

"You will be reunited with your betrothed soon," he assured her as he picked up her garments from the floor.

Miss Wrenwood shrugged as she rose from the bed. "I met him but once when we were in leading strings. I have no attachment of consequence to him."

She stepped into her shift. Dominic helped her into her

corset.

"He is a fortunate man to have such a fine prospect for a wife," said Dominic as he laced the ribbons of the corset.

"Will you ever marry?"

Dominic paused and the vision of Adanya flashed before him. Marriage seemed an absurd idea, but the thought of spending the rest of his life with Adanya by his side was not unwelcome and felt more than right.

"Pirates are not the kind to marry," he said.

"I envy her freedom."

"Captain Mbwana? Freedom is what she hopes to secure for others. She was one of the fortunate ones."

"Mr. Withers told me that you rescued her and her father off a slave ship."

"Aye. Her father rescued me back. I would have had a sword through my heart were it not for him."

"And you love her?"

Dominic paused. How was it that women could detect such things? He thought about his first encounter with Adanya. He had felt an odd sense of shared destiny with the urchin who had launched a stone at his groin. That he was able to find her years later, floating in the middle of the ocean, could only be the work of some greater Providence.

"It would seem we were fated to be together," Dominic replied.

When he had finished the last of her buttons, she faced him. "I could make a fine wife for you if you wanted."

Dominic smiled and brushed away a tendril of hair from her face. "You would not want to. Life aboard a ship is harsh. Life with a pirate is worse, my love."

"My betrothed will not want me when he discovers that my virtue was taken."

"You are a beautiful woman, Miss Wrenwood. He would be a fool not to have you. And if he is a fool, you would not want to have *him*."

He kissed the top of her head and watched her leave. It caught him by surprise that she had developed such tender feelings for him. Miss Wrenwood and Adanya differed as day from night, but there was no question as to whom he wanted at his side. He needed a woman of strength and fortitude. He needed Adanya.

Where was his quartermaster? Dominic wondered after Miss Wrenwood had left. He was impatient to have Adanya in his arms again. This time he would have her in his bed and explore every part of her body, trailing fingers and lips along her jaw, under her chin, down her throat, over her shoulder. He wanted to feel the softness of her lips beneath his and tongue the crevices of her mouth. Tenderly caress her mons. Grind hips in a slow and scintillating dance.

"About bloody time," said Dominic when he heard a knock at the door.

The quartermaster was not alone. He was accompanied by Rowland and the boatswain.

"We come to let you know, Captain," said Rowland, "that a vote be taken."

Dominic's face darkened. A vote that he was not a part of was not a good sign. He raised his brows and waited for Rowland to elucidate.

Rowland lifted his chin as if to better look into Dominic's face even though he was the taller of the two. "We wish to collect the bounty on Captain Mbwana."

Dominic clenched a fist. This would be the second time he felt like killing his first mate.

"A vote by whom?" Dominic asked, staring at each of the men in turn. His quartermaster and boatswain looked away.

"The entire crew," Rowland answered. "Sixty-four in favor."

His heart sank. That meant even those who knew Captain Mbwana when she was simply Adanya had voted to turn her in. "Why was I not consulted?"

"You hardly seemed impartial, Captain," Rowland said, unable to keep the sneer out of his tone.

Dominic eyed the man's throat, imagining his own hands about it. The blunderbuss would deliver too quick a death for this man.

"We reckon you either be with us or..." Rowland continued.

"Are you threatening a mutiny, Mr. Stirling?" returned

Dominic, the vein in his neck pulsating fiercely.

"Twenty thousand quid be an awful lot, Captain Bold," his quartermaster piped, as if that fact could temper the insult of a mutiny.

"It would not take us many raids to secure an equal amount."

"Aye, but this be right easy. No lives need be threatened. We have simply to give her up at the nearest British port."

"And you trust the British to reward pirates?"

"No harm lost if not."

Suppressing the facial muscle that threatened to twitch with his fury, Dominic responded, "Then let us make for the enemy's den."

Chapter Ten

The last time she had chains about her, she had been part of the cargo imprisoned below deck, allowed a glimpse of the sun only when forced to exercise above deck twice a fortnight. Chained like mongrels, fed like sows from the same trough, and spat upon like vermin. Living in the stink of their own refuse. Death was sanctuary, for the hell awaiting them at journey's end might prove ten times worse.

Adanya stared at the iron cuffs about her wrists and the chain that ensured she could travel no farther than the bars that held her prisoner. They had taken the dagger she kept about her thigh and left her with only a bowl of rancid water. Even if she could break free of her chains, there were the bars and the guard to contend with. The guard, a large and hairy man burnt red by the sun, grinned at her like a dog eyeing a bone.

"Be your bars so weak that they must post a guard to watch me?" she asked him.

"You be worth a hefty sum—wouldn't want nothing to happen to ye," the orangutan replied and flashed his decaying teeth at her.

The door of the hold opened.

"Adan—Captain Mbwana."

The guard scrambled to attention. "Captain Bold, sir."

A wave of relief washed over Adanya. Finally Dominic was here to put an end to this. She would gladly witness the punishment Dominic was sure to put to Mr. Stirling.

Dominic looked the guard over from head to foot. "I require a word with the captive—alone."

The man shook his head. "Fear I can't do that, Captain. Mr. Stirling gave strict orders that I never let the captive outta me sight."

Dominic took a step closer to the man. "Once we have delivered Captain Mbwana to the British, do not think that I will forget this act of insubordination."

The orangutan looked conflicted. "Mr. Stirling said I would lose me share of the bounty if I fail to keep watch."

"You will lose more than your share of the bounty when I am through with you."

Adanya could see flames in Dominic's eyes. She had witnessed only a few crew members incur the wrath of Dominic, and they had paid dearly at the end of the cat-o'-nine-tails.

"Have a heart, Captain," the orangutan pleaded. "Mr. Stirling thought ye might bear tender feelings toward the captive—or such."

Dominic gave him a half smile. "Mr. Stirling knows little of me. Since when did wanting a taste of quim mean I've any feelings of the tender sort?"

Her eyes widened. Had she heard him correctly?

The orangutan shared a lascivious smirk. "Aye?"

"And I have tasted many a quim, have I not? I assure you hers is particularly delightful."

She opened her mouth to speak, but no words emerged. Had she imagined the moment she had shared with Dominic but a few hours ago?

"But no quim is worth more than twenty thousand quid," Dominic continued as he eyed her. "Still, one can enjoy her a while longer, eh? Hand me the keys."

The guard gave Dominic the keys and looked on eagerly. Dominic opened the cell door and walked in.

"Yer a fuckin' bastard," Adanya said as she backed away from him, feeling her heart break for the second time. How could she have misjudged him so?

"I be a pirate," he explained, continuing his advance. "Do you expect me to pass on a prize such as this?"

He was within arm's reach. When he took another step towards her, she made a feint to her right as if to escape to his left, then swung both her arms up towards his face. Her fist glanced off his jaw. He stared at her in surprise, then grabbed her chains and hauled her against the cell wall. He pinned her wrists above her head.

Leaning in, his mouth next to her ear, he whispered, "Adanya, listen—"

But she was struggling too wildly to hear. "Take your bloody hands off me!"

She unleashed a torrent of invectives then brought her knee to his cods. Dominic grunted and doubled over. She rushed past him, but he grabbed her chains and pulled her to the ground. She rolled over and delivered a swift quick to his shins. He stumbled.

"Bit of a hellcat, ain't she?" voiced the guard as he looked on with delight.

Dominic smiled without releasing her from his gaze. "The fair sex play at these games, but make no mistake, they desire to be caught."

This was not the Dominic she knew. Five years had transformed the man to a stranger. She wanted to cry. Had she the opportunity, she would grieve for the man she once knew. This man standing before her now had betrayed her. And yet she had succumbed to him, had lain next to him thinking that he cared for her. What a devil's fool she had been. A bloody fool.

When Dominic took a step towards her, she spat at him. She would rather be touched by a slave trader.

He wiped her spit from his cheek with the back of his hand. "You would kill me if you could," he observed.

"Happily," she seethed.

"You had your chance," he said. "Pity you chose to fuck me instead."

In fury, she lunged at him. He stepped aside and pushed her to the back wall. Her cheek pressed painfully against it. He came up behind her and pulled the chains up between her legs, cleaving her mons and nearly pulling her feet off the ground. She yelped and struggled in vain to break free.

He murmured into her ear, "For God's sake, trust me, Adanya."

The sound of her name tempered her thrashing. It was the way he said it. The stranger was gone. It was the voice of Dominic. The man she had loved. Still loved.

"Fight me, Adanya," he ordered.

Her heart was already hammering in her chest. Now her mind whirled as she tried to comprehend what he was saying.

"I need you to fight me," he reiterated.

Still confused, she remained motionless.

In a loud voice that the guard could hear, he said, "Have you surrendered then, my dear?"

He yanked her breeches down below her buttocks. This galvanized her into action, but try as she might, she remained trapped between his hard body and the wall.

He lowered his voice and whispered in her ear, "Where does your ship make berth?"

"I'll not breathe a word of it to you," Adanya muttered. How could she be sure if it was Dominic or the stranger who spoke?

"Indeed?"

His hand snaked around her hips and two fingers grazed her clitoris. She inhaled sharply. No. She could not surrender. Not again.

But an old familiar throb began between her legs as his fingers brushed and fondled her. Her legs threatened to buckle.

"Where would the *Sea Falcon* be?" Dominic attempted once more.

She whimpered. She felt his cock stiffening and hardening against her back. His fingers slipped against her slit. Oh God, she was wet.

"Trust me, Adanya," he pleaded softly into her ear.

Her eyes snapped open. She couldn't afford to trust him.

She stamped as heavily on his foot as she could. He let out an oath. Instead of retreating, he shoved her farther into the wall and hastily opened his breeches to pull out his cock.

"Aye, teach her a lesson, Cap'n Bold," the orangutan said.

She cried out when she felt his length filling her. She had been unprepared for the manner in which his cock stuffed her quim. And yet, it felt wondrous.

"Where, Adanya?" Dominic whispered, drawing out his cock

languidly.

Adanya moaned. "Tortuga…"

Dominic shook his head and thrust his cock back in her forcefully. "Don't lie to me."

Despite the presence of a third person, she felt herself giving in to the ripples of pleasure that fanned from her quim to the ends of her limbs every time Dominic moved in and out of her. His hips met her buttocks in a rhythmic movement. She felt lightheaded, as if from an opiate. It was awful how much he could command her body.

"Try again," he instructed.

"An unnamed island…" she mumbled.

"Where?"

He had slowed his tempo. She bucked against him in the hopes of maintaining the tide.

"Where?"

This time he withdrew completely, taking the wind from her sails.

She whimpered, her quim grasping at emptiness. "Due west of St. Kitts…"

He plunged back into her. His fingers strummed against her clit. She cried out as her body shook with convulsions.

When she came down from the heavens, the world was still spinning. She barely heard Dominic whisper, "Await my word."

He let her gently to the ground, fixed his breeches, and walked out her cell, closing the door behind him. She peered through the haze and saw that the guard had brought out his own cock and was stroking it vigorously. Dominic threw the man back the keys.

"Her cunnie is mine," Dominic told him. "Lay a hand on her and I'll see you keelhauling at the end of a rope."

The guard grumbled and pulled his pants back up.

It wasn't until her breathing came easily that she realized Dominic had left her the key to her chains.

Chapter Eleven

W e make for the coast of St. Kitts," Dominic informed his navigator and pilot.

Rowland looked at the map before them with skepticism. "Barbados is much closer."

"Aye, and more closely guarded. There is likely to be more of His Royal Majesty's Navy about those waters," Dominic reasoned. "We have only to find the local magistrate to serve as our messenger. We deliver Captain Mbwana only on our terms."

The quartermaster nodded his head. "It is the sensible course."

"That is why *I* am captain," Dominic finished as he stared at Rowland.

After the navigator and pilot had plotted the fastest course, Dominic returned to his cabin. Keeping his anger in check before the traitors of his crew took an immense amount of control, and Dominic was glad to be rid of company. He needed to remain calm for Adanya's sake.

He had not meant to ravish her in her cell—merely pretend to do so. But his cock had a mind of its own when in her presence. Like a shark sniffing the scent of blood in the water, it reared its head whenever she was near.

She probably loathed him right now. He wanted nothing more than to seek her company and assure her that all was well, but he refrained from visiting her the next few days lest he arouse suspicion. He did, however, speak to Mr. Withers, who had gone so far as to accuse Dominic of cowardice and demanded that those loyal to Adanya take arms against the rest.

"Our numbers are too small—we would all die," Dominic

had responded, "and Adanya would swing above the low mark as sure as the tide."

"Then what are we to do?" Withers bemoaned.

Dominic had put a reassuring hand upon the older man's shoulder. "Ensure that Adanya remains healthy. See that she gets a ration of salted beef and rice. Leave the rest to me."

The night before they were to reach St. Kitts, Dominic allowed an extra ration of rum to be served to the crew to celebrate their anticipated bounty. The men drank heartily and toasted each other often. A crewman took out his fiddle, and they sang of treasures and fair damsels to be had. Dominic joined in the revelry until the men had either taken to their hammocks or fallen asleep where they drank.

The moon had begun its descent when Dominic crept into the hold where Adanya was kept. The guard was sitting on a barrel, snoozing in the corner. Dominic covered the man's mouth and drew his blade against the man's throat. He lowered the guard to the floor and grabbed the keys to unlock her cell.

"I was beginning to think ye had changed your mind," Adanya whispered as she took the cuffs off her wrists.

Dominic grabbed her shirt front and brought her mouth to his in a long and dizzying kiss.

"Never doubt me again," he advised before releasing her. He handed her a spare cutlass. "Withers awaits starboard in a dory."

Adanya nodded and followed him up the steps. Under the cover of dark, they made it to the side of the ship. Withers had already prepared the boat. Miss Wrenwood and the doctor were with him.

"Get in," Dominic instructed. He followed Adanya into the boat.

"What are you doing?" Adanya demanded, eyes wide. "You're not coming."

"You'll need more than Withers and Robbins to row you ashore. It won't take them long to discover the guard dead and you missing."

"But...the *Phantom*..."

He didn't have time to explain that he would give up his ship and more for her. Gesturing for her to be silent, he helped to lower the boat into the water. Then he took up the oars. Everyone grabbed a paddle to aid in the effort.

They rowed for hours. It was not until the sun had peered its crown over the ocean waves that they spotted gulls in the sky.

An ache like a smoldering flame filled the muscles of his arms and back, and despite having removed his shirt, he continued to sweat. Adanya stayed with him every minute of the way, perspiring as profusely as he, though he had insisted that she take a rest. Her response had simply been, "I be me own captain now."

He smiled through his fatigue. That she was.

The boat scraped sand, and though Dominic felt like collapsing onto the beach, he instructed Mr. Robbins and Mr. Withers to look after Miss Wrenwood while he and Adanya looked for the *Sea Falcon*. They would then make accommodations to take Miss Wrenwood to the nearest colonial governor to return her to her betrothed.

"We make berth over the hills there," Adanya directed.

They walked in silence along the beach, each in their own thoughts with only the gentle rushing of the waves to grace their ears. The sun crept slowly towards its zenith when Adanya finally broke the quiet.

"The *Phantom* be your ship for nigh on a score."

It was a statement but meant as a question. She wanted to know why.

"Aye," said Dominic and looked at her askance. "She was my greatest love—once upon a time."

She stopped in her tracks. Her bottom lip quivered. They stared at each other, willing the rest of the world to fade.

"I never took your gold, Dominic," she said. "I would never have stolen from you."

He took a step towards her and put a palm to her cheek. "I don't care if you did."

Her eyes began to water, making the whites of her eyes shimmer in the sunlight. He realized, though he had rescued her from the life of a slave, he had enslaved himself. Her tears, her smile, her body would keep him in bondage forever.

"Though there be the matter of a wager you lost while aboard the *Phantom*," Dominic said with a wry grin.

Her eyebrows rose. "*I* lost? I think it *you* who lost."

"Perhaps. It doesn't bloody matter now."

He lowered his mouth to claim her. She kissed him back with an ardor stronger than he had ever felt. She circled her arms about his neck and pulled him further into the vortex of renewed love, of five painful years melting away, of her heat and desire for him. His kisses began tender and became increasingly demanding as his tongue probed the crevices of her mouth. Their tongues met, and it seemed they each drew strength from the joining of their lips.

"Adanya, Adanya," Dominic murmured into her neck as he trailed kisses to her collarbone and pushed her shirt down her shoulders. She had worn the shirt loose, leaving the neckline open all the way to her waist, half of her breasts exposed to view. Even as he had summoned all his strength to continue rowing, he had felt his cock stiffening despite the company of the others in the rowboat.

They sank into the sand where he covered her body with his. The blood was pounding in his head and his loins. He wanted to make love to her slow and sweet and make her spend a dozen times. He pushed aside the linen and pulled out one ripe breast. He circled his tongue around the hardened nipple, sucked it, and bit it while she writhed underneath him, arching her back, pushing her breast farther into his assaulting mouth

Suddenly Dominic felt a hand in his hair and he was pulled to his feet, then thrown back to the ground. A heavy boot pressed down upon his neck. The point of a sword flashed before his eyes. Dread filled him as he wondered if his lust had brought about their death.

"Damon!" he heard Adanya call.

"Captain Mbwana."

"For God's sake, let him up."

"Eh?"

"Do as I command!"

It seemed the man pushed harder down on his boot before

releasing Dominic. Rubbing his neck, Dominic rose swiftly to his feet to see a muscular blackamoor with ten other men, all African.

"We saw the boat come into the island. We thought he be ravishin' ye, Captain," said the one named Damon.

"He was," Adanya said with narrowed eyes. "This be Captain Bold of the *Phantom*."

Dominic made a curt bow. Grunts of acknowledgement were exchanged, though most of them received him with only a hard stare.

"An honor, Cap'n Bold," Damon said with reserve before turning to Adanya. "Yer a might fine sight for the eyes, Cap'n."

"As are you, Damon, though I owe you for the blow to me head."

"I should be glad to take what punishment you would bestow, Cap'n."

"How fares the *Sea Falcon*?" Adanya asked.

"She be needin' repair."

"How long before she can be put to sea?"

"Four more days, mayhap three."

"Good." She looked at Dominic. "We've a ship to reclaim."

He smiled. God, how he loved this woman.

"There are three on the beach where we landed. See that they are treated well," she continued, her eyes never leaving Dominic. "I shall see the rest of you back at the ship. Captain Bold and I have unfinished matters."

Dominic felt the skeptical gaze of the first mate upon him, but he didn't care. For him, the men couldn't leave fast enough.

When they had left, albeit reluctantly, she sidled up to him and smiled into his eyes. The blood coursed through his body, desire raging from his cock to every limb, a need to devour her.

"Where were we, Captain Bold?"

Dominic swept her into his arms. Her legs wrapped about his waist. He took her many times on that beach, bringing her to ecstasy with his mouth, his hands, and his cock. The endurance of his own desire surprised him, and he spilled his hot seed into her equally hot wetness until there was nothing else to spend.

The sun gave way to lesser stars. And in the moonlight they finally rose to make their way to the *Sea Falcon.* He wrapped an arm about her waist. After years at sea, he had found the greatest treasure of all. He had claimed his pirate.

THE END

Submitting to the Baron

Chapter One

Leopold spencer, the fifth Baron Ramsay, felt the blow in his groin, as if one of the steeds currently rounding the straightaway had kicked him in the bollocks. He lowered his field glasses and tried to address his friend with calm. "Where is it you say our wives are staying?"

"Château Follet," Charles responded a little louder over the noise of the grandstands. "Or some demmed Frenchie name. By Jove, the Turk took that turn well! I think my judgment of horseflesh can finally rival yours, eh?"

Though the Royal Ascot meeting was the purpose of the day for Leopold, with the Gold Cup yet to follow on Ladies' Day, a more important matter now held his attention captive. Charles knew not that Château Follet was also known by the name of Château Debauchery, or he would not have spoken of the place with such indifference.

"Your wife, Diana, told you this?" Leopold asked.

"Yes, she was rambling away, as wives will do, about which shops and millineries they would patronize whilst in London. Dreadful dull matters that can only interest the fair sex. I told her that, with enough changing of the horses, she could make the trip to Town in one day, but she thought the journey might prove too taxing for *your* wife. Said that this Château Follet was the perfect place to spend the night—possibly two, as she is well acquainted with the lady of the house."

The impish little vixen. Leopold felt his groin tighten. It surprised him little if Diana, his cousin, knowing full well her husband never listened to her with more than half an ear, should deliberately flaunt the name of Château Follet, a den of debauchery where men and women engaged in taboo pleasures of the flesh. He had not thought Diana would return there after marrying Charles. Though Leopold had always enjoyed his visits to Follet, he had forsaken the place after marrying Trudie two years ago.

Good God. Trudie. Was she aware of what transpired at the Château? It was too incredible that his shy and awkward wife should know of, let alone venture into, such a place. The wicked wantonness there would surely horrify her.

Of a sudden, he recalled an unremarkable conversation between them at the breakfast table a fortnight ago, when Trudie had announced that she and Diana wished to travel to London to purchase fabrics for the latest fashion plates.

"As—as you and Charles will be at the races," Trudie had said, the pitch of her voice higher than usual, "we ladies will have a bit of our own fun in Town."

He had nodded and politely inquired where they were staying and the length of their stay, though, in truth, he had been more interested in returning to his newspaper at the time.

"I—we—Diana has arranged the, er, particulars."

She had not met his eye and was instead fixed upon applying a fifth coat of jam to her toast. Trudie had none of the guiles that many others of her sex perfected. Her eyes of cornflower blue, often wide with naiveté, could hold no falsehood. She was artless, a quality the late Mrs. Spencer had often extolled in recommending Trudie Bonneville to her son. The eldest of three, Trudie was also responsible and sensible. Leopold respected all these traits.

And found them rather dull.

But perhaps Trudie was not as sensible as he would have thought. They had been married two years, though, as his mother and hers were the best of friends, he had known Trudie since she was in leading strings.

When he had gone off to Eton and then Oxford, he had seen little of her during her maturation into a young woman. Nonetheless, as she still possessed the rounded cheeks of her childhood and appeared no more comfortable in the attire of a woman than she did in the lace-frilled gowns her mother used to always adorn her with, he saw the same girl who would hide behind the sofa with a plateful of biscuits, unaware that the powdered sugar masking half her face betrayed what she had been about.

He never would have selected Trudie for himself—she was middling in appearance and wit—but it was his mother's dearest wish before her death to have the two families united.

"I think your luck has taken a turn for the worse, Leo," Charles said with a nudge. "Your horse has fallen half a lap behind."

Leopold looked out over the tracks. His steed did appear to struggle, but losing a hundred guineas was hardly important now. He cursed himself, for, as he reviewed the days prior to his departure for Ascot, to be followed by his wife's departure for London the following day, he now saw that Trudie had been ill at ease all those days. She had hardly looked him in the eye. Though she was prone to fidgeting, as if the pins in her gown poked her constantly, she could hardly sit still at the dining table. She ate quickly and often asked to be excused.

The greatest evidence of her nerves, however, lay in her favorite pastime, the pianoforte. Trudie excelled at the instrument and could play for hours. He knew her to be attempting a new concerto—the one in C Major by Mozart, he believed—but she had been unable to play through pieces that she had mastered years ago.

Her odd behavior had not attracted his notice at the time, but now he viewed it with great foreboding, for why would she display such disquiet lest she well knew what Château Follet was about?

He had not thought to hear its name again, though Diana had once teased him, suggesting that the *four* of them could have a ribald time there, but he had quickly quelled such a notion. Trudie was far from comfortable in the bedchamber. Their wedding night had been quite the disaster for both of them. He had been as gentle as he could, and she had tried to contain her cries, but it was evident to him that she took no pleasure in their congress. He had hoped, after the initial pain, that subsequent attempts would prove more agreeable to her, but she had looked ready to leap from the bed at his every touch.

She would never engage in any of the activities at the Château Follet. Surely Diana, one of her dearest friends, knew this? The two women talked often, and their sex had a habit of leaving no subject unturned.

But then why were they headed to Follet? What could Diana intend but to make cuckolds of him and Charles? He knew Diana to be discontented in her marriage, but would Trudie acquiesce to adultery? He would not have thought it possible, but as he reflected on the past sennight, she had been behaving with all the indications of a guilty conscience.

Granted, he himself had not been faithful in the last year, though he did not brandish his affairs as Charles did. He was not a poor husband, in that he never spoke a harsh word to Trudie and always treated her with courtesy and kindness. She knew as well as he that their marriage served to satisfy their families. Their mothers had crafted their engagement at their births. The Bonnevilles had wealth, and the Spencers had breeding. Both families benefited from the match.

The excitement of the crowd rose, with Charles cheering loudly, as the horses came into the final lap. Leopold glanced at Charles, wondering if he should inform his friend of the need to depart Berkshire immediately to rescue their wives. Charles would be livid and want to lock Diana in her chambers, perhaps more cross at being pulled away from the races than at his wife's infidelity.

Leopold decided he could fetch the two women and bring them home himself. The responsibility to inform Charles would then rest appropriately with Diana.

It was a good day's journey to Château Follet, but if he departed within the hour, he could arrive before the women had to spend the night.

Charles leaped in triumph as the horses crossed the finish line. "Damn me, the Turk won! He won!"

After celebrating with the fellow beside him, who had made the same fortunate bet, Charles turned back to Leopold. "Here now, I know your horse finished down the field, but you look as if you lost more than a hundred quid. The day is young. You may recoup your losses yet. Lest your wife overspends her allowance, eh? I know Diana will with hers."

Leopold managed a grim smile. "I shall have to take my losses for the day. I fear I have neglected a matter that, upon reflection, requires some urgency to resolve."

Charles stared at him. "Eh?"

"Make my bets for me while I am gone and keep the winnings if there are any to be had."

Knowing this to be an offer Charles could not refuse, Leopold took his leave. He ought to trust that Trudie, once she realized what Château Follet was about, would turn upon her heel in an instant to seek safer shelter. Surely Marguerite Follet, the proprietress, would see that Trudie was not a suitable guest.

But he could not risk it. And, perhaps, locking one's wife in her chambers might yet prove an appealing option.

Chapter Two

Leopold paced the anteroom of Marguerite Follet's boudoir. Little had changed since last he had stayed at the Château Follet some years ago. Despite a palpable nostalgia for the place, he was far from happy over the circumstances that currently compelled his presence. The roads to Château Follet had been favorable, and he had made good time, but throughout the journey he had felt the impending cuckoldry in the depths of his loins. Diana may not have provided specifics to her description of the château, but she could not have expected to conceal its purpose from Trudie. Given his wife's recent behavior, it was more than likely she had agreed to the affair. Leopold had inventoried all the men Trudie knew. None appeared the obvious offender. If she had been unfaithful, she had hid it well, though he had never known her to be deceitful till now. He knew the hypocrisy of condemning Trudie for her faithlessness when he himself entertained a mistress, but her choice of the Château Follet for her tryst riled for reasons he could not name.

"She should not be here," he insisted to Madame Follet after being admitted to her room.

The proprietress stood in her negligee while a chambermaid assisted with her toilette. Though his senior by many years, Madame Follet wore her age with grace and elegance, aided by eyes that sparkled with vigor, a smooth and pale complexion, and a trim figure. She narrowed her eyes at his hasty speech.

Recalling his manners, he quickly bowed and kissed her hand. "Your pardon, Madame. *Comment allez-vous?*"

"Leopold Spencer," she remembered, her gaze sweeping over him with obvious appreciation of what she saw. "*Je vais bien.* Now, of whom do you speak?"

"My wife."

She raised a brow. "You are not arrived together?"

"She came without my knowledge."

"Lost the reins to your wife, have we, Lord Ramsay?"

He bristled.

"Rather a surprise," she continued as she examined the different pairs of stockings offered by the maid. "I remember you as quite the *dominant*."

His hand twitched. He would have gladly returned to the Château if he had thought his mistress receptive to the experience. Few women had the inclination and fortitude for Château Follet.

Marguerite lowered her lashes. "As you know, we've plenty of leashes here."

"My marriage is not that sort of arrangement," he said, though the thought of clapping a leash on Trudie was not wholly objectionable, especially if she were inclined to run off on wild and irresponsible ventures.

"How unfortunate. I know not your wife, but she must be the flaxen-haired young lady who arrived with your cousin?"

"Were they accompanied by anyone or did they rendezvous with another guest?"

"I am not aware of their plans, *mon chéri*."

"I want them sent home."

"Lord Ramsay, you may take up the mantle of master with your wife as it pleases you, but do not require my intervention."

"They know not what they are about. This is no place for Trudie," he maintained, and began to pace once more.

She looked at him sharply. "I invite all manner of women to enjoy themselves here."

"I meant no offense, Madame, but I think my wife to be entirely naïve as to what transpires here. Château Follet is beyond her."

Marguerite sat down at her vanity and began applying her powder. "A bold insistence by someone caught unawares of his wife's whereabouts."

"Trudie is the last person I would expect to find here."

"It would seem that you do not completely know your wife."

A muscle tightened along his jaw.

She looked at him through the mirror. "If you mean to rescue your wife from the treachery of Château Follet—"

"Madame, you must know I have only fond recollections of my time here, but Trudie is...inexperienced."

"If you wish to claim her, I shall not prevent you. But the hour is late and you have but arrived. My groomsman Jacque is at your disposal, and there are many guest chambers available. I invite you to make yourself comfortable. You are welcome to stay the night—or two. I do believe Diana and your wife are staying at least two."

At least *two?* he nearly bellowed. Instead, he said with comportment, "I am honored by your invitation but, regretfully, I cannot accept."

"Are you so certain the women will go with you?"

"I cannot force Diana to leave with me, but I will take my wife."

"And install her under lock and key so that she never returns?"

Leopold squared his shoulders. He had not yet pondered that possibility. A proper scolding should dissuade Trudie from ever considering a second visit to Follet...but what if it did not?

"Madame, will you not explain to my wife—"

"*Certainement no.* You would ask me to criticize my own residence?"

"I beg your pardon! That is not what I intended. I only meant that you could, with your vast experience, dissuade Trudie and convince her that she would find Château Follet most unsuitable."

"But I know not your wife. And I will say to you what I said to an overbearing marquess last week: that I find it rather selfish of you to deny her the pleasures that you have partaken readily of here at Château Follet."

Her words jolted him, especially when he had considered himself quite magnanimous for not condemning his wife her infidelity. His intention in coming to the Château was to *protect* Trudie.

Marguerite softened her tone. "Given your absence from the Château, perhaps you should consider making up for lost time. It would please me much if you chose to stay."

She held out her hand, a clear signal of dismissal. He pressed his lips to her hand. There was little to be done but accept her offer for the moment.

Ensconced in one of the guest chambers, he dismissed Jacque soon after the groomsman had assisted him out of his coat and boots. He went to the sideboard and poured a glass of brandy. He finished the beverage rather quickly, then poured himself another. He gazed at the painting on the opposite wall. Scantily clad nymphs, many with their nipples showing through their thin garments, danced with satyrs in a forest setting.

He settled into an armchair facing the four-post bed. His last time here, he had a lovely maiden tied between those posts, moaning and writhing with delight to his skill with the crop. His surroundings and the brandy sank in, warming his blood. A shame he would not be able to partake in the events of the Château. But his mission was clear.

It was unfortunate that Marguerite was not willing to accommodate his request. Who better than the proprietress herself to convince Trudie of the inappropriateness of the Château? And she would have spared Trudie the embarrassment of facing her husband, though he took some gratification at the thought of witnessing his wife's mortification. Surely she would think twice about deceiving him and running off to places such as the Château Follet!

Now he had no option but to remove Trudie from the château himself. If he marched himself into her chambers, she would be too surprised and shamefaced to protest. But, as he had voiced to Marguerite, there was no guarantee that Trudie would not simply return at a later time.

He glanced at the longcase clock opposite him. The hour was indeed late. He had no affinity for traveling at night, and it would be too dangerous for a woman. He could claim his wife now, before any of the evening's activities took place, but he admitted a growing curiosity to know the extent of her infidelity and whether she would truly consent to the debauchery here. He could not imagine Trudie would tolerate the extreme and sometimes violent nature of the carnality when she could ill handle the overtures of her own husband, but it had been over a year since he had approached her. Perhaps it was best to keep a furtive profile and depart on the morrow. He could keep an eye on Trudie to ensure her safety *and* discern who her possible paramour might be.

He rose and went to the armoire. Opening its doors, he found a selection of face masks. He picked a simple half mask of black satin. A matching black banyan hung beside it. The lighting at the Château was always dim, but he chose a powdered wig to further disguise himself from recognition.

As he donned the articles, he felt a strange anticipation.

Chapter Three

His wife was nowhere to be found.

"Are you quite certain she is not in her chambers?" Leopold inquired of the maidservant he had asked to search the rooms.

"Yes, m'lord," the woman replied.

"But her effects are still there? She has not departed?"

"Her portmanteau remains unpacked."

Leopold returned downstairs to the assembly room, where the pairing ritual was held for guests to claim their partners. He saw Diana upon the lap of a handsome rogue, and thought of Charles joyfully watching the races, oblivious to his wife's infidelity. Engrossed in murmuring into her paramour's ear, she took no notice of Leopold. Even if she had, she would likely not have recognized him behind his mask and wig. He was tempted to ask Diana, who ought to have, as she had brought Trudie here, looked after her friend.

"Was she here?" Leopold asked of Madame Follet, who sat with her legs stretched upon a sofa while a young man several years her junior held a glass of wine to her lips.

"I've not seen the baroness since supper," she replied after a sip. "I do hope she is well and can partake a little of the pleasures of the night. I would have tended to her more, but since you are here, I thought it unnecessary."

"Are all your guests accounted for here?"

She looked about the room. "I think a few have left to begin the true start of their evenings."

Leopold knew not how to receive the information. When first he had entered the assembly room earlier to see with whom Trudie might engage in criminal congress, he had been relieved to find her absent. Perhaps she had come to her senses and had chosen instead to retire for the evening. That she was not in her chambers left open the possibility that she might have gone off with one of the guests. It concerned him. She could not possibly fathom what transpired here at Château Follet, even if Diana had provided the most detailed of descriptions. Hearing of the activities was not the same as suffering them.

And what of the man who would serve as her dominant one? Would he be kind and gentle? Would he perceive her awkwardness and how easily she could be discomfited?

Leaving the assembly room, Leopold renewed his urgency to find Trudie. As he went through empty room after empty room on the first floor of the château, he began to consider how he might search the bedchambers upstairs without bursting in upon unsuspecting guests, but there was no way to prevent such an event if he was to be thorough in his search. And he would not rest until he had found Trudie.

After he discovered her safe and unharmed, he would be tempted to give her the proper scolding she deserved. It mattered not if she had come to Château Follet at Diana's urging. In coming, Trudie had acquiesced to committing adultery. She had acquiesced to making him a cuckold.

His anger should be tempered, he knew, by guilt over his own infidelity, but wives could not be made cuckolds. He had done his duty in marrying Trudie, had treated her with nothing but kindness, had seen that she had more than enough in the way of pin money and had never denied her anything of consequence. That he did not often visit her bed was likely a relief for her. And she would repay all this by making him a cuckold.

As he allowed his anger to stew, he heard music coming from behind the partially closed doors of a drawing room. Looking through the opening, he beheld a woman seated at a pianoforte, her back to him. Like him, she wore the fashion of the prior century. Her satin dress of dark indigo had petticoats that made her full hips appear even more ample. Her hair was done in a powdered coiffure, but he recognized her figure.

Entering, he stood at the threshold and listened. A skilled

pianiste, Trudie often liked to challenge herself with difficult pieces. At present, she played the "Sonata in E-flat Major" by Joseph Haydn. The large composition reflected much of the composer's late complexities and sophistication. At the instrument, she commanded a passion that did not appear in her demeanor. Or perhaps he had simply not noticed it before.

She finished the final notes with flourish. Having been engrossed in the music, she nearly fell off the bench at the sound of him clapping. She scrambled to her feet and nearly knocked the bench over. She steadied the seat before standing behind the far end of the bench. Though she wore a Venetian mask over her eyes, he knew by her movements that it was Trudie.

"You're an accomplished player," he remarked in low, hushed tones to disguise his voice.

"Th-Thank you," she replied. She pulled at the sleeve of her gown, where layers of lace descended from the elbow. Knowing his wife, she could not be comfortable in such a garment. She adjusted the mask as she cleared her throat.

"Do you await someone here?" he asked.

"No, I—I passed by the room quite by accident and saw this instrument, a Broadwood, and I could not resist."

He eyed the beautifully grained rosewood and mahogany beside her. In addition to its stately harpsichord case, the instrument produced more resonance than the Viennese she had at home.

"The other guests are gathered in the assembly room," he said.

"Yes, I know."

"If you are alone at the château, you may acquire a partner there."

She drew in a sharp breath and nodded.

"But you must hurry," he added. "Some of the guests have dispersed already."

"Thank you, but I think—I think I shall retire for the evening."

He was relieved but raised his brows. Could she possibly have come for no reason other than to keep Diana company?

"Retire? The night is young yet."

"Yes, well, I had a rather long day of travel."

She scratched at her hair, and he imagined the powder to itch considerably. It would have been no easy task to outfit herself in the fashion of Marie Antoinette. Why undertake all that effort for naught?

"Nevertheless," he replied, "one does not venture to Château Follet to *rest*."

His comment made her uneasy. She seemed not to know where to look.

"I did not think I would feel as fatigued as I do," she answered at last. He could tell she was perturbed by his prodding but was too polite to call out his impertinence.

"Then you did have, at least, the intention to avail yourself of the offerings here."

"Your pardon?"

"This must be your first visit to Château Follet."

"Yes. It is a lovely estate."

"May I ask how you came to know of it?"

"My friend. She is acquainted with Madame Follet."

"And she told you what transpires here?"

Trudie stared at him with brows knitted. Undoubtedly, she was trying to place the motive for his questioning. "Yes."

"Are you acquainted with anyone else here?"

"If—if you will not find me rude, sir, I do think I should retire."

She waited for him to respond, but as he did not move, she remained where she was.

"Your friend left you to fend for yourself?" he tried.

"Did Madame Follet send you, sir, to inquire after me?" Trudie replied.

"She was concerned that you would not enjoy yourself properly."

She let out the breath she held. "Please tell Madame that I much appreciate her hospitality but regret that I cannot avail myself of the, er, festivities offered."

"Why not?"

"I find myself fatigued."

He caught the irk she tried to keep out of her tone. "Is that all?"

"Sir, I am in earnest and will bid you good night."

If he were to act the gentleman, he would bow and step aside. She was waiting for just such a motion, but he remained where he was. Upon stepping into Château Follet, one divested the mantle of gentleman and lady.

Flustered, Trudie looked about as if seeking another means of escape. Unaccustomed to wearing such voluminous petticoats, she tugged at her skirts. She stopped. "Will you not miss the pairing event yourself, sir?"

Leopold grinned to himself at her attempt to rid herself of him. "I have no interest in the pairing."

"Oh," she responded with disappointment before deciding to ask an impertinent question of her own. "Why, then, are you at Château Follet?"

"I came to retrieve something of mine."

"Ah, well, I pray you will convey my apologies to Madame Follet, and, as the hour is late for me—"

"You're married," he said, directing his gaze at her wedding ring. He had taken care to remove his when changing.

She thrust her right hand over the left. "I understand it to be of little consequence here at the château."

"None," he affirmed. "Nonetheless, you must be discontented in your marriage to come here, lest you came with your husband."

Her bottom lip quivered. He had clearly touched a nerve.

She squared her shoulders. "What marriage is not touched by discontent?"

Her response, though arch, lacked conviction. He took a step farther into the room. "So your husband is not here. Have you a paramour here?"

She retreated a step. He could see her mind churning to find the appropriate response. He had never known Trudie to prevaricate—till recently—and a less mannered woman would have called him out for his prying.

"No," she answered. "Did Madame Follet request these questions?"

It was not a poor attempt to put him in his place. Finding her response rather droll, he took another step forward. "I merely think it curious that one would come all this way to Château Follet and *not* partake of its purpose. Do the activities frighten you?"

She retreated a step. "A little. They are...beyond what I am accustomed to."

"But they interest you."

"My friend persuaded me that it would be a fine experience."

He pressed his lips into a line. It would seem she had, at one point, considered her participation at Follet. "Do you believe her?"

Trudie faltered. "Sir, you ask questions of a rather intimate nature."

"You were ready to submit yourself—your body—to a perfect stranger. My questions are harmless in comparison."

He should have been relieved that she had opted to go to bed instead of pursuing a liaison, but he found himself wanting to know how far she would have gone if she were not fatigued as claimed. He advanced another step.

"Do you believe your friend?" he tried again.

"I believe—I believe her knowledgeable in these matters," she said. "She has been here before and praised the enjoyment of it."

"And you wished to sample the pleasures here for yourself." At her guilty expression, he felt both a wave of sympathy and anger at her willing betrayal. "Worry not. As one who has indulged in the offerings here many a time, it would be hypocritical of me to censure you. Indeed, I praise your pursuit of the fleshly pleasures. Much courage is required, particularly of your sex."

Her countenance softened. "It—it would have been an adventure unlike any for me."

"The adventure can still be had."

She fussed with the lace at her décolletage. He eyed the lush swell of her breasts and felt a tug at his groin.

"Perhaps, after a cup of tea or coffee, you can overcome your fatigue," he said. "Why come all this way to return empty-handed?"

She did not refute his reasoning and lowered her gaze in thought, but then she shook her head. "I could not."

"Why not?"

"I know no one here."

"There can be much titillation in lying with a stranger."

"Yes, Dian—my friend said the same."

"And you are inclined to believe her, are you not?"

"But I am married."

A muscle rippled along his jaw. That had not stopped her from coming to Château Follet, but he kept his tone friendly. "Your husband does not note your absence?"

"He enjoys the races at Ascot. He would not miss me."

The latter sentence was murmured as if to herself, but he heard the resignation in her voice. "Indeed?"

She seemed surprised that he had heard. "Yes, well, he—he has a mistress to satisfy him."

It was his turn to be surprised. He had not known that Trudie knew. He had taken care that she would not.

"Are you certain of this?" he asked, searching her countenance for emotion. Was she saddened or vexed by his mistress? To his surprise, he found neither sorrow nor anger but a calm acceptance of his infidelity.

She nodded. "My friend—her husband made mention of it to her quite by accident."

Charles. Leopold suppressed an oath. He should have known Charles had as large a mouth as Diana.

"Hearsay does not qualify as verity."

"Well, I—I saw her—his mistress, that is."

"How unfortunate," Leopold said carefully, "that your husband should flaunt his mistress before his own wife."

"Oh, he did not! I arrived at London last season a day earlier than I had told him I would. When I was told he had gone to the theater, I followed suit and saw him—them. She is quite pretty. Beautiful, rather."

Stunned, Leopold stared at her. His wife had lied to him more than once? What else had she hid from him? Seeing the sadness now in her eyes, he put aside the queries for now. He cursed himself. He had hoped to spare Trudie the pain of knowing—had even convinced himself at one point that she would hardly care that he had a mistress because she had demonstrated so little interest in the amorous attentions of her husband. Many a husband entertained mistresses, and their wives either did not know or chose to look the other way.

But a part of him had always known such attempts to convince himself of the harmlessness of what he did to be false. He had feared that Trudie would be hurt. If she had been more receptive of him in bed, he might not have felt as compelled to take a mistress. But it mattered not how much fault could be placed at her door. He could not rid himself of the remorse.

"I can see why a man, wed or not, would wish to keep her company," Trudie said wistfully.

Behind his mask, Leopold winced. Her words were a dagger that twisted the guilt inside him.

"Then it is only fair that you indulge in your own liaison," he pronounced.

She stared at him as if contemplating his reasoning. "I—I suppose."

"What stays you?"

"Oh, I think I am not quite ready."

He advanced toward her, wanting a better look into her eyes. "What does your readiness require?"

She took a step back for every one he took towards her. "I...I know not. Well, it does not matter."

"Why?"

He was at the piano bench, and she was near the wall. He had not spoken with firm conviction when declaring that she matched her husband's adultery, but he was becoming more assured that perhaps two wrongs could make a right, of sorts.

"Well, I—the pairing is surely over by now."

"Madame Follet can make arrangements. There are always the manservants. They are all handsome. You could easily avail yourself of one."

Not realizing she had come up against the wall, she stepped backwards and bumped into it. "Oh! I think not."

He took another step toward her. She could have slid to the

side and escaped his nearness, but she seemed at a loss, like a cornered mouse.

"Why not?" he demanded.

"I..."

He had drawn up before her, and she looked rather alarmed. "Sir..."

"Why not?" he asked. The image of his wife beneath one of the rugged young bucks flashed through his mind, and he found he still balked at the notion of becoming a cuckold. But if a liaison of her own was what she desired, perhaps she deserved to have one.

"It is—they...please."

He had closed the distance between them. As he leaned toward her, he could not keep the edge completely from his tone. "They *what?*"

She seemed to tremble. "They—they would not desire me."

He stopped.

"I am hardly a beauty," she supplied.

Unlike others of her sex, she did not reproach herself in search of compliments. She spoke with sincerity. He looked her over from head to toe. Though his wife had not the slender figure admired by most, she had a womanly suppleness to her form and other qualities to recommend her: the brightness of her eyes, the evenness of her teeth, and an unblemished complexion. He took a curl of hair and drew it before her bosom to lay upon a swollen mound.

"You underestimate your desirability, madam," he said.

She drew in a sharp breath and appeared at a loss for words.

"Perhaps," he continued, "as we are both without partners, I could oblige your purpose in coming here."

Her eyes widened, and an unexpected desire to assert his command caused heat to flow through him. How would she react if he took her into his arms right now and kissed her? Curious to know, he reached for her. Before she could object, he had wrapped his arm about her waist and drawn her to him. His mouth descended upon hers.

She gave a muffled cry and pressed her hands against his upper arms, but her resistance was weak. Her lips were softer than he remembered, and they yielded quite nicely beneath his, causing the blood in his veins to course more strongly.

He parted her lips to taste the interior of her mouth. Her stiffness began to thaw as he roamed the orifice. Her powder, rouge, and the scent of something he could not name filled his nose. When he lifted himself to allow her a breath, he could see her mind swimming. She blinked but seemed unable to focus her eyes. The flutter of her thick lashes and the heaving of her bosom called to a primal urge within him. He lowered himself to claim her mouth once more.

This startled her into motion. She slid away and managed to stumble toward a settee in the middle of the room.

"Your offer is a kind one," she turned to say, while taking steps backward toward the egress, "but perhaps another time."

He advanced toward her. "You wound me, madam."

Her face fell. "I-I do not mean to suggest that I do not desire to be with you. It is that..."

Sweet Trudie, he thought to himself. She always did concern herself with others.

"You fear me," he filled in for her.

"I cannot say. I hardly know you. I think it is that I doubt myself."

"Doubt yourself? Permit me to show you there is no reason for it."

She hesitated, and this was all the time he required to cover the distance between them. He caught her arm and pulled her to him.

"Come," he urged. "You came to Château Follet with one intention. Let us fulfill it."

Chapter Four

He tightened his grasp on her. One hand held her arm; the other was at the small of her back, pressing her to him. Her struggles were timid, as if she feared too much resistance would be impolite. She could fall into the submissive role all too easily.

"Is this not what you seek, my dear?" he murmured into her neck. As his lips grazed her, he felt roguish and wicked, but he could not desist. It was not merely charity or a desire to bolster her vanity that compelled his seduction. An unexpected titillation manifested in the charade he played. To his surprise, he found he wanted to possess Trudie for his own.

She gasped, leaning away from him, away from his lips. Her hands pressed against his chest, but they did little to keep him at bay. He moved his hand to her upper back. His head lowered over her chest, he kissed the small indenture at the base of her neck. Her cry turned into a groan.

His cock throbbed. Had she always felt this lush in his hands? Always smelled this enticing? Or was it the prospect that she had intended to give herself to another man that suddenly made her more alluring?

Jealousy was a common device used by women to encourage more affection from their lovers, and he abhorred the tricks that such women employed. But Trudie had no wiles. Yet she had intended to commit adultery without his knowledge. He knew not which he preferred.

He kissed the area about her collarbone then trailed lower, to the tops of her breasts. "Come. Let us realize the intention of your journey."

She could have done more to hamper his advances—slap him, strike him, claw him—but she either knew not how or had no wish to. He did not doubt that his wife had never before found herself in such a situation, being manhandled by a stranger. She had no practice in such affairs.

Her effort to distance her bosom as far as she could from his preying mouth pushed her hips at him. He could feel her skirts surround his legs. He pressed his pelvis toward her. She leaned too far back and lost her balance. They stumbled backwards, but he guided their fall toward the settee. Now she was trapped.

He saw fear shining in her eyes—but also the glow of arousal. Blood surged through his cock.

"Please," she tried once more, like a mouse pleading to a cat for mercy.

He paused, his conscience willing him not to torment his wife. But how many men had an opportunity to ascertain the strength of their wives' fidelity? A part of him still hoped she would remain true to her marital vows, but her crimes might lessen the guilt he felt. And his seduction must surely flatter her.

He had one leg between hers, and the other knelt upon the settee against the outside of her thigh. She could not escape unless he allowed her.

"Please, what?" he inquired. "All I do is what you desire me to do."

He dropped his head and softly kissed the side of her neck. She did not fight him this time, and her dramatic breaths were not wholly the result of exertion. They held anticipation, too.

"No," she said feebly as he continued to nestle her neck. "I think—I think I erred in coming here."

"Allow me to show you that you did not."

She moaned when he put his hand upon a breast and gently slid his palm where he thought the nipple to be. He wanted the orbs bared, but her attire did not aid in his seduction. He continued to caress her neck and her décolletage till her neck arched over the back of the settee. She had a lilting pant. For the most part, she had avoided his gaze, but when he moved his hand to her ankle, she started.

"Shhh, there is naught to fear," he assured.

But her body had stiffened in alarm.

"What did your friend promise you would happen here?" he asked to distract her.

"Acts of d-depraved debauchery."

"And this appealed to you?"

"She—she said the desires of the fair sex do not differ from men, though we are taught to believe otherwise."

"Do you agree?"

She lowered her eyes farther. "I am not without lust. I suppose I am a weaker member of my sex."

He grasped her chin and lifted her gaze to his. "Desire is as natural to our bodies as hunger. You need not be ashamed. At Château Follet, these desires are exalted and fulfilled without censure. Avail yourself of the most sublime pleasure. I vow it will rival Mozart's finest concerto."

An avid admirer of that composer, she looked a little incredulous, but he was up to the task of proving his assertion.

He lowered his head to claim her mouth. She gave a muffled protest, but then her lips parted beneath his, permitting him to taste her fully. The heat in his veins flared. Her resistance had not completely dissipated, but he was glad for it, because it enabled him to apply greater pressure. With his hand upon her chin, he manipulated her so that he could sample her mouth at a variety of angles.

She inhaled sharply when he delved his tongue into her.

Despite the newness and perhaps the strangeness of having her orifice assaulted in such a manner, she sighed, barely protesting when he smothered her mouth more fully. Consumed by his kiss, she seemed not to notice his hand slipping beneath the hems of her skirts and sliding to her knee. But when his hand touched the bareness of her thigh, she yelped against his lips. She squirmed.

"I mean only to pleasure you," he murmured.

"But—"

He took her lips into his mouth, quelling her protests. Surprised to find her mouth so intoxicating, he was content to stay his hand while he kissed her long and hard. Only when he had felt her yield significantly did he move his hand to the inside of her thigh.

"Hmph," she mumbled when his hand had reached the apex and then the outset of her folds.

The devil. She was not merely damp. She was near sodden. When he nudged the flesh, she became frantic, and tried to wriggle away as if she meant to clamber over the back of the settee. He stayed her with a hand upon her shoulder.

"Calm yourself. I promise it shall not hurt."

"I am not—I am not prepared for this," she gasped.

"Prepared? My dear, this is not a concert. You have but to lie back and enjoy what I am to do."

He pressed his thumb at the nub of flesh between her folds. She cried out at the contact, her body bowing off the settee.

"We must not..."

Her words turned into a moan as he circled his thumb against her, slowly coaxing sensations both exquisite and torturous. Her eyes rolled toward the back of her head, and she grasped the settee as if in immense pain. He marveled at how strongly her body reacted, and when their gazes met through their masks, he glimpsed the fear he had seen in her on their wedding night. He had been too bewildered by it then to do much about it. But tonight would be different. This time he would show her the proper conclusion.

Her lips moved, but her words were lost. She squeezed her eyes shut, and it almost seemed as if she were not enjoying his fondling, but her wetness continued to flow. Her breaths grew haggard. His forefinger took a turn next, stroking that sensitive bud.

"Surrender yourself to the pleasure," he encouraged, sensing that she still fought the delicious tension. "Naught but ecstasy awaits."

His touch was still gentle. If he had been with his mistress, he would have been agitating his entire hand against her as she ground herself into him.

"Oh my, oh my," Trudie pleaded between clenched teeth.

With his fingers, he continued to build that beautiful tension from which one desired to topple. He hoped it would be so for Trudie. Her brow furrowed, and her groans and grunts increased. He sensed her arousal, but still she seemed to oppose the bliss that awaited her. He considered if his tongue might prove more effective, but such wantonness might startle her too much.

He intensified his fondling, making her legs quake. Her groans sounded slightly of sobs. Alarmed, he ceased his ministrations, but instead of looking relieved, she appeared vexed and even more distraught. She whimpered. He resumed his caresses. He would show her the end was well worth the present agitation.

Eventually, something inside her seemed to shatter, and her body went into violent paroxysm. Her cries pierced his ears as she bucked beneath him, her limbs jerking and flailing. He had never seen her spend, and was in some wonder of it. He had never seen any woman spend in such fashion, with such vigor. Desire pumped through him to the tip of his cock. The prospect of all that he could do with her filled him with excitement.

Chapter Five

With her cheeks flushed and her brow smoothed from satisfaction, Trudie looked beautiful. Her lashes fluttered, and when she opened her eyes, she gazed at him as if from a blur—but then he seemed to come into focus and she started. When Leopold bent to kiss her again, she put up her hands and tried to push him away.

"I must go," she blurted.

"We have only begun," he replied, still leaning toward her.

She pressed her hands against his chest. "No—I must."

She sounded more insistent this time, but her reservations had melted easily enough before. The swelling at his crotch grew tight at the thought of making her spend once more and in finer fashion.

"There is more pleasure, greater pleasure, to come."

She tried to slip from under him, but he, not being done with her, kept her body pinned to the sofa.

"Please," she gasped between her struggles.

Was she presently overcome with guilt? It was too late now. He reached between her legs. She tried to close them and push his hand away, but he persisted until he had reached that nub of flesh between her folds, still deliciously swollen and wet. She quivered. It was as he thought.

"No..." she moaned, but despite her protest, a radiance shown from her eyes.

With one hand, she attempted to yank his out from between her thighs while her other hand continued to push at his chest. Her squirming only caused his blood to heat further. Still wanting another kiss, he lowered his head. When her efforts gained her no traction, she shoved at his chin.

He grabbed the offending hand and pinned it to the sofa. "Do

you not wish to spend again and more gloriously then before?"
he asked.

"I must not." She spoke as if trying to convince herself.

He fondled her, but she became more vigorous in her
struggles.

Why did she wish to stop now? Now that his cock was hard
as flint and yearned for release?

"I promise you an ecstasy your body has never before
known," he murmured against her lips, recalling how sweet
and yielding they had been.

"No! I-I have sinned enough."

Her despair ought to have stayed him, but a faint hesitation
hung about her words. He felt sorry for her remorse, but if she
had not wished to be unfaithful, she should never have come to
Château Follet. It was true she had resisted his seduction at
first, but she had eventually succumbed. And spent. She had
never spent for her husband before but had done so now at the
hands of a stranger, a circumstance Leopold now found vexing.
A surprising jealousy flared within him.

"It is of no consequence now," he said. "You have made of
your husband a cuckold already."

She slapped him across the face with her free hand, taking
him by surprise. Was he the offender? After she had so
willingly submitted herself?

He grabbed her second hand and crushed his mouth atop
hers, muffling her scream. In her attempts to throw him off, she
unwittingly pressed her body to his crotch several times,
tempting the hardness there. Dispensing with his earlier
tenderness, he probed her mouth roughly. The blood pounded
in his head, drowning out his conscience. She was, after all, his
wife. She should not be giving away what was rightfully his. As
her husband, he was merely claiming his prerogative.

Her strength was no match for his. She kicked her legs,
pressing her feet into the sofa to provide some leverage to free
herself from beneath his weight, but his pelvis kept her pinned.
He ground himself into her as his mouth continued to assault
hers, his tongue probing into her moist depths. A part of him
did wish to make her regret coming to the Château, but he was

mostly overcome with a desire to possess her, to prove that she was his and no other's.

She twisted her head to escape his brutal kisses. Sensing she would not relent, he knew of one way to wear down her resistance. He let go of one hand and reached again between her legs once more.

His touch sent her into a frenzy. She pushed at his face. But the effect of his fondling was immediate, quieting her vigor.

"Please, sir," she pleaded, her protest akin to the soft mew of a kitten.

"I promise your body will know the divinest pleasure," he said, teasing and tempting the seat of her desire.

She shook her head weakly. "It is enough. Please."

But she had ceased to claw him and her body trembled beneath his. He plied her clitoris, leaving her panting anew.

"You are ready to spend again," he noted, his head swimming with the scent of her arousal.

"No."

He almost laughed at the feeble rebuff. He slid a finger into her slit. With a loud gasp, she grabbed his upper arm. The look upon her countenance called to his cock. He sank a second digit into her. She groaned. Her lashes fluttered. He curled his fingers and gently stroked.

"Dear God," she whispered, her eyes wide behind her mask, which sat askew as a result of their scuffle.

Her arousal was ripe, sensual, exciting. He wondered that he had not had the patience before to discover the beauty in her pleasure.

Trudie dug her fingers into his arm as his digits fondled her with a little more vigor. The wet heat of her cunnie was marvelous. If they were in the proper way of Château Follet, he would make her beg to spend. He withdrew his fingers and straightened to undo the buttons of his fall. His cock sprang free, stiff and ready. She stared at it, frightened, as if it were a weapon that could hurt her.

"I will be gent—" he began.

But she had sprung off the sofa and scrambled for the doors.

He caught her and they tumbled to the ground. She clawed

and hit at him, dealing a fairly decent blow to the side of his head before he could grab her wrists and pin them to the floor.

"How unkind of you, madam. You would take pleasure but provide none in return?"

She paused briefly but resumed her resistance. Once again, her struggles only fueled the lust inside him. He had thought to prevail in his seduction, and was surprised his skills had not brought about her complete surrender. She did not understand that his cock was the superior fit for her cunnie, and that she would enjoy it much more than she had his fingers. He would show her how superb it would feel.

"You will find a more amenable woman," she protested, "one who can satisfy you better."

Recalling how easily she had dismissed herself earlier, he held her gaze in his and said, "It is you I want."

Her eyes lit up yet she continued to waver. "But..."

"Is this not what you had sought in coming here?"

She whimpered, her indecision arousing his earlier turmoil. He had a right to claim her, and his cock would be satisfied with nothing less. He wanted to show her that she was desirable. He was also cross with her for being so easily seduced by a stranger, for seeking to commit adultery. With his knee, he nudged her legs apart. He released one hand to pull up her skirts. She took the opportunity to strike at him and nearly knocked his mask off.

Stifling an oath, he flipped her onto her stomach and held her down by putting a knee to her lower back. He untied his cravat and used it to bind her wrists behind her.

"You brute!" she cried, flailing with the desperation of a fish out of water.

"You came seeking debauchery in the form of criminal congress," he reminded her. "I am merely fulfilling your intentions."

He threw her skirts over her waist, revealing plump and unblemished buttocks. If he had more patience, he would've stopped to admire them more, but his cock would wait no longer. More swiftly than he'd intended, he sank his length into her.

She gave a long cry but lay still, allowing him to savor the glory of her cunnie. He thought she would take to screaming, and he would have reconsidered his actions if she did. Instead, she whimpered.

He reached a hand around her hip, past the voluminous skirts bunched about her waist, and nestled it at her groin. His fingers found her clitoris. Her moan was long and low.

Fighting the urge to shove his entire shaft into her, he concentrated on strumming that swollen bud between her folds. She shook her head and whined a little, but he could sense her resistance melting away as more and more wetness coated his fingers. He pushed a little more of himself into her. She felt divine.

With his hand beneath her, theirs was no easy position, but he fondled her to the best of his ability. And when he had sheathed his entire cock inside her paradise, it seemed she gave a welcoming groan. He did not fault her for succumbing. There was little she could do, and a part of her must find it flattering that a man desired her enough to ravish her.

The wet heat surrounding him was irresistible, and he began a gradual thrusting. She squirmed, and he shoved deeper to keep her in place. He intensified his fondling of her clitoris.

"Oh my," she murmured.

With Trudie, it was not unlike having congress with a virgin. Her cunnie was deliciously tight, and he was satisfied that it was so because no other man had spread her legs before. He was now steadily pumping in and out of her, his pelvis slapping against her rounded rump. She grunted between uneven breaths and muttered unintelligibly. It was undoubtedly an uncomfortable position for her, being pressed into the hard floor with her arms pinioned behind her and her legs spread. But this was nothing compared to what the women at Château Follet were accustomed to enduring. Nevertheless, Leopold silently promised her a gentler coupling next time.

"I grant you permission to spend," he said.

Her grunts became cries. A few minutes later, her cries culminated in a wail, and her body fell into that familiar paroxysm. She shuddered beneath him, and it was enough to send him over the edge to join her in carnal rapture. His cock erupted, draining the tension that had built in his cods and groin. Delicious shivers racked his body as he spent more violently than he could remember. With a roar, he bucked and trembled against her till he had emptied the last of his seed into her.

When the explosion had settled into a hum in his body, he slid out of her and collapsed beside her to catch his breath. He closed his eyes, still in amazement at the splendor of it all.

Realizing her hands were still tied, he propped himself up and undid her bonds. She rolled onto her back and stared up at the ceiling. He took a hand and kissed it. "I pray you spent well?"

She said nothing at first, and he worried that he had been too rough with her.

"I did...thank you," she said at last.

Relieved, he lay down and looked up at the ceiling with her. Various emotions still warred within him, but he came to a decision.

He would stay a while at Château Follet after all.

THE END

ABOUT THE AUTHOR

EM BROWN is an award-winning multi-published author of contemporary and historical erotic romance. She found the kinky side to her writing after reading stories at Literotica.com. She likes to find inspiration from anywhere and everywhere, be it classical movies, porn, embarrassing high school photos, her favorite Sara Lee dessert, and the time she accidently flashed an audience with her knickers.

For more wicked wantonness, visit www.EroticHistoricals.com.